WINTER RULES

By the same author

Laid Dead
Unnatural Hazard
Dead Ball

Barry Cork

WINTER RULES

CHARLES SCRIBNER'S SONS
New York

Maxwell Macmillan International
New York   Oxford   Singapore   Sydney

First United States Edition 1993

Charles Scribner's Sons
Macmillan Publishing Company
866 Third Avenue
New York, NY 10022

Macmillan Publishing Company is part of the Maxwell Communication Group of Companies.

Library of Congress Cataloging-in-Publication Data
Cork, Barry.
    Winter rules / Barry Cork. — 1st U.S. ed.
        p.   cm.
    ISBN 0-684-19506-2
    I. Title.
    PR6053.O687W56   1993   92–18035   CIP
    823'.914—dc20

Macmillan books are available at special discounts for bulk purchases for sales promotions, premiums, fund-raising, or educational use. For details, contact:

Special Sales Director
Macmillan Publishing Company
866 Third Avenue
New York, NY 10022

10   9   8   7   6   5   4   3   2   1

Printed in the United States of America

For
Anne, Christine and Patrick

THE ROGUES GOLF CLUB

Thornton Basset

Winter Rules

As from October 31st a ball lying on any close mown area through the green may, without penalty, be moved, or lifted and cleaned and placed within six inches of where it originally lay, but not nearer the hole.

Signed G. D. H. L. Blunt
Secretary

CHAPTER 1

All great cities get by with very little sleep, catnapping fitfully for an odd hour out of the twenty-four, none of them the same. New York slows to a fitful standstill between half past three and four in the morning, Paris a little after three, which is a couple of hours later than Amsterdam. Common sense tells one that the still hour of any metropolis is dictated by finite things, such as the time bars shut, the last train goes and just when the early trucks head in to stock tomorrow's markets. Sentiment doesn't go along with that, preferring to think of the city yawning like a sleepy woman and pulling the bedclothes over her head. For me, I find the phenomena no more than a useful clock, so that when silence fell that night outside the flat in London's Kelvington Mews I knew without looking at my watch that it was precisely half past two.

Half past two and a clear winter morning. Samuel Pepys, scribbling his diary three centuries ago, would have listened to the cries of the Watch making its round. *Half past two of a fine morning and all's well.* I rested my elbows on the desk and just listened to the silence. My mind was very nearly a blank. Really if one couldn't sleep it made more sense to read a book than write one. Or, as in the present, write about one.

'And when you've got a moment,' Laurie Wilson had said, 'Eleanor asked if you'd mind doing your own biography bit for the *Pride of Lions* jacket.'

Laurie was my agent, Eleanor Henderson the editor at Hanwick and Jameson who published the results of my part-time literary endeavours. Between the two of them they had me organized much to their liking, even to the

writing of my own potted life story to accompany the
usual blurb on the turn sheets of the book's dust cover. It
was only a few lines but for some reason it was a job I
disliked intensely.

'What's wrong with the one they used last time?' A token
protest, no use. I knew I'd end up by doing the thing in
the end.

'New book, new bio, I suppose. All you have to do is
shuffle it around a bit.'

I studied without enthusiasm my effort so far.

*Angus Straun was born in St Andrew's, Scotland, in 1953, and
educated at Fettes and Edinburgh. At one time had hopes of becoming
a professional golfer but joined the police force instead. He wrote his
first best-selling novel* Blood Debt *while recovering from a gunshot
wound sustained on duty.*

Curious how false-looking the truth could be, with the
dodgy bits left out. Perhaps I should have given the thing
to Laurie to write. I thought the idea over and tried
to imagine quite what Eleanor Henderson would have
got.

*Straun insists that his writing is no more than a spare time
occupation and refuses to give up his police job, despite informed
advice to the contrary. Wastes most of his royalties on running a
ludicrously expensive Italian sports car. Prepared to take quite
unnecessary physical risks, but a moral chicken. One failed marriage
and he's scared senseless at the mere thought of making the same
mistake twice.*

Well, maybe the last bit was less than fair. My marriage
to Angela may well have been a disaster but it had at least
left me with a half share in my eight-year-old son, Sam.
And Laurie? The objective assessment of the early hours,
when things tended to be down rather than up. Laurie was
asleep in the next room with my half of the bed growing
cold beside her. She was good at her job, good with Sam,
good with me. She was tough and sexy and funny and I

was in love with her but I was still wary of her potential as a wife. Laurie was my agent, my literary adviser, who hawked my wares and led me through the intricate mine-fields of rights and contracts. I enjoyed writing and I enjoyed the research it entailed, but I liked being a police-man, too. As things were at present I could do both, but if Laurie was my wife I wasn't so sure.

Away over the rooftops a single late taxi on quadruple fare negotiated Hyde Park Corner, an unmistakable diesel clatter that chuntered away up Knightsbridge, faded and died. The world reverted to quiet. Well, comparative quiet, certainly not complete. A metallic something? I put my pen down and listened consciously and was half sure I'd picked up the sound again, muffled through the drawn curtains. I switched off the reading lamp and engulfed myself in total dark. The desk was against an inside wall and my back was to the window, but it was a small enough room and I was unlikely to get lost. A something that hadn't been there a moment before hit me across the shins. A chair. I swore at it and pushed the thing out of my way.

'Darling, what on earth are you *doing* out there?' Laurie wasn't a plaintive woman but like the rest of us she wasn't at her best on being woken up.

I said, 'I'm falling over a bloody chair. Go to sleep.' The great lover, always there with a ready answer. But my eyes had accustomed themselves to the darkness and I could make out the outline of the window. I wondered what was making me so cautious about a few sounds that might very well be no more than a prowling cat. Sixth sense? A sixth sense is for wild things, not environmentally battered urban dwellers. City policemen were lucky to be left with the same nerve ends as anyone else, let alone any extra. All they got in exchange was experience, perhaps not all that bad a trade. I edged the curtain aside and looked down at the sleeping mews.

Behind me, Laurie said, 'What is it?' Her voice was close, quiet now and awake.

I said, 'I'm not sure.' Directly below me was the pleasing bulk of what my accountant was pleased to call Straun's Folly, the car which the illustrious firm of Maserati had named the Khamsin. For anyone it was what the media boys call a statement and even for a slightly odd police inspector somewhat over the top. Occasionally, such as when I paid the servicing bills, I had qualms, but that was no more than a momentary weakness and easy to suppress. Only men with mean souls equate money with five litres' worth of Italian automotive genius, a thing of beauty and a source of infinite pleasure. Admittedly my Maserati did not come cheap but I'd earned the thing by the sweat of my typewriter, so what the hell.

Laurie moved silently beside me. 'Someone after the car?'

'I think so.' He'd had me fooled for a moment, whoever he was, with his body motionless in a patch of shadow, but then he'd moved and I'd spotted a crouching figure, fiddling with the car's nearside door. 'Saucy sod.' The easy condescension of the law-enforcer for the unblessed, the predator for the easy kill.

'I told you it was asking for trouble, leaving that thing out there.'

I said absently, 'I know.' Her Golf lived in her new flat's single pint-sized garage which in any case couldn't have accommodated the Khamsin, a quart-sized car if ever there was one. But daft to leave the thing outside, right enough.

'Are you going to ring the police?'

There was something about the way the shadow was leaning against the door that I didn't like. Locks are not particularly expensive but damaged door panels cost the earth to repair and I'd seen some of the horrific damage done to cars by mindless vandals intent only on getting their grubby hands on a radio set. 'You ring,' I said.

'They'll radio the nearest patrol car—' I paused, caught up with a picture of whichever PC had answered the call. *Might I have your name, sir?*
And this is your address, sir?
Oh, I see, sir. Then whose address is it?
I winced. Who said the British gentleman was dead, when he was clearly alive and suffering in London SW1? Very probably Laurie wouldn't have given a damn but my Scots forebears were fretting. Traditionally one simply didn't put a lady in a compromising situation, thereby tarnishing her good name. There were also practical considerations, come to that, because I can't say I exactly relished the happy chat back at the station when the word got around.

'No,' I said, 'don't ring. It's only some idiot youth wanting a joyride. I can cope.' I closed the curtains again and turned back into the room.

Laurie looked unhappy. Her fair hair was tousled and without the big reading glasses she looked about sixteen. For some reason she'd pulled on my old towelling bath robe, a garment that was several sizes too large for her, and the whole thing was very sexy in a Lolita-ish kind of way. Who was I kidding? It was very sexy in any kind of way.

She said, 'Angus, please don't be a fool. Wait for the police.'

Woman's unfailing belief that any Little Man, however incompetent, is a better bet than her own. No wonder, I thought, doctors don't treat their own wives. Chance would be a fine thing. One could imagine a senior surgical registrar trying to bandage his wife's cut finger. *Darling, don't you think we'd better call a proper doctor?* I said, 'I *am* the police, for Christ's sake!' and went downstairs in a huff.

In the minute hallway I paused. The door was secured with a Yale plus a deadlock and by the time I'd got those open whoever was outside would be half way to Brighton.

On the other hand, whoever had converted No. 42's original carriage space into a garage and hallway had taken advantage of the fact that he was dealing with the end of the row. Back in the days when mews were mews it had been possible to walk a horse round the side of the building to a small space at the back, where presumably some esoteric equine business had been carried out in the minute cobbled yard behind. That yard had now been converted into a trendy patio approached by its own door. I glanced down at my feet and checked that I was wearing the ancient, soft-soled moccasins in which I habitually slopped about the house. They looked eminently suitable.

I went out the back door into the bright moonlight of the London night.

It took only a few seconds to cross the tiny garden Laurie had made, and I padded silently up the side of the cottage and paused at the corner before sneaking a look round. As it happened, there was no need for caution, because by now my quarry had the Maserati's door open, a picture of concentration as he fiddled with the ignition. I drifted on through the shadows and paused again. Conveniently, a couple of fire-engines sped across Hyde Park Corner, whining and snorting through the gears as they made for Piccadilly, and under cover of the noise I circled whoever it was and came up behind him. The inevitable jeans, trainers and black flying-type jacket. Well, what else?

'All right, son,' I said amiably. 'You're nicked.'

He must have heard the words a few times before because he knew exactly what he was going to do, and he didn't hang about getting started. Without bothering to look up, he came out of the car backwards, his right elbow jabbing back like a battering ram.

I'd guessed what was coming the moment the black jacket started to come closer, so the elbow caught my hip instead of my stomach, and even there it hurt. There is a fashionable school of thought that considers a reasoned approach in such circumstances is desirable, in case some up-and-coming villain's feelings may be upset. Oh well. I put both hands behind my client's head and shoved his face against the edge of the car's roof.

I said, 'Watch it.'

He had a look at me then, and in the moonlight I had an even better look at him. Short, curly ginger hair. Freckled. Clean-shaven, fortyish. Five feet ten and solid, now with a cut over one eye where the car roof had caught him. He looked old for a standard tearaway, but not so old that he didn't enjoy hurting people. Something odd, too, about the eyes.

'All right, man,' he said, 'you bloody asked for it.' A faint accent, hard to place.

He got the knife out with remarkable speed, and I heard the slam of the spring-loaded blade locking fast and he came straight in. Every day, something new to learn. In my experience knife-wielders tend to wave the thing around in front of them, both to show that they've got it and to strike a suitable degree of fear into the enemy. But this chap clearly didn't hold with that and no more did I. On film it's good and easy to seize an attacker with a crafty bit of kung-fu or whatever, but they do things differently in Kelvington Mews at two o'clock in the morning. I jumped sideways to avoid the thrust and found it was my turn to have the car behind me. I vaulted hurriedly over the bonnet. Head first, he came after me.

And I didn't like that. I didn't like it at all. There is something very off-putting about someone compulsively doing the wrong thing, and diving straight over the Maserati's bonnet like that was very wrong indeed. Sensibly, if you can call a flick-knife attack sensible, he should have simply chased me round the end of the car, keeping his feet firmly on the ground, and if he wanted to be athletic

he'd have done better to follow me feet first, with arms
and knife ready for action. To dive at me, offering himself
momentarily prostrate, was the act of a mad dog. I resisted
the temptation of that unprotected but doubtless very hard
head and instead grabbed his knife arm by the wrist and
yanked it up, letting the momentum of his body pull it
backwards. It should have dislocated his shoulder at the
very least but it didn't, which was an interesting example
of the difference between theory and practice. The knife fell
out of his hand, though, and he landed in a bundle at my
feet. Unless you happen to be wearing heavy gloves, beating
people around the head does little damage to anything
except one's hands, so as he got up I hit him hard but
carefully, flattening his nose and adding further damage to
his bad eye. He gave no indication of even having felt the
blows. The eye I could still see was fixed on me with a kind
of inhuman intent and at the back of my mind alarm bells
began to ring. This man was frighteningly strong. More to
the point, he showed a pretty considerable desire to get to
grips with me for the sole purpose of tearing me apart.

A desk for you from now on. Thus the president of the medi-
cal board that had left me to languish in administration for
five years. Well, a blast from a bank raider's sawn-off shot-
gun hadn't done my right shoulder a great deal of good.
Now I could swing a golf club reasonably again, but brawl-
ing for real was asking a lot from patched-up muscles.
Ginger pounced towards me rather in the manner of a cat
who has decided he's been fooling around with a mouse
long enough and I wished heartily that I had some kind
of weapon handy. A pick-handle isn't recognized as being
within the Queensbury rules but one would have been a
considerable comfort just the same.

The gods denied me a pick-handle but someone up there
must have decided to help out because at that moment
Laurie chose to drop a flowerpot in the direction of my

assailant's head. She missed, of course, but the flash of red earthenware-potted geranium startled us both as it flashed before our eyes in the moonlight and smashed itself to pieces on the cobbles at our feet. But it gave me an edge, because I realized immediately what the thing was, whereas Ginger didn't. Instinct, self-preservation or whatever, literally forced him to stop dead in his tracks and look up to see where it had come from. Well, it was the only chance I was likely to have, so make the most of it. I hit him about four inches above his belt buckle with everything I had, twice.

I don't know how much it hurt him. Probably not very badly because it felt remarkably like banging one's fist into a well-padded mattress. But he grunted, all the same, and had a look at me with something approaching interest. Perhaps he thought that he would find it more fun taking me apart if I showed a certain amount of life. I thought gloomily that it was pointless blaming wear and tear for my performance. Maybe I'd been tougher once than I was now. But I also knew with uncomfortable clarity that at no time in my life could I have put this one down. Ginger shifted his feet in pleasurable anticipation, but before he could start in on me there was the bang of a hastily raised sash window and more light splashed down on us, like floods illuminating a stage.

'Angus, do get out of the bloody way!'

I looked up. Ginger looked up. From the upstairs window of the highly prestigious double cottage on the far side of the mews my neighbour, and publisher, Sir Charles Plantagenet Brown, was leaning out flourishing what appeared to be an elephant gun. Of Hungarian extraction, the elegant Charlie was liable to go off at half-cock over minor matters of commerce, and I had no wish to discover how he reacted to a physical confrontation. Neither for that matter did I particularly see him in the dock on a charge of blowing

Ginger apart. I rather rashly stood in front of my attacker and waved the gun down.

'For God's sake, Charlie! Put that thing away!'

Charlie Brown hesitated, but at least he didn't pull the trigger. Behind me there was a scuffle. Ginger was staring at the drainpipe barrel pointing down at him with considerable dismay, which was understandable. Apparently enough was enough, because suddenly he waltzed sideways round my car, turned and then did what may have been obvious but was certainly the last thing I'd expected him to do. He simply dived into the car and slammed the door.

I suppose I stared at him for about a second. It wasn't long, but long enough for him to lock himself in and, by the time I'd grabbed the handle, the engine was barking into life—either a duplicate key or a neat bridging job had got the car going. Only just time to let go before the Maserati pounced forward, rear wheels spinning on the cobbles. The back end snaked savagely as the power came on, then the car reached the end of the mews, swung left and was gone.

'Do you think you might make a *little* less noise?'

Thus Lady Chelson, Laurie's next-door neighbour, a voice easily identifiable without looking up.

'Sorry,' I said. The flowerpot had undoubtedly made rather a lot of noise, to say nothing of the sounds of battle. If I'd had any sense I'd have asked someone to throw down another couple of geraniums but fortunately it wasn't necessary because another, even more distinguished window opened and a male voice made itself heard.

'—or I'll ring the bloody police!'

I stood for a moment, looking after the car, trying to get my breath back, thankful for the sudden quiet in Kelvington Mews. Though not all that quiet, because from somewhere over my head Laurie's stage whisper was suggesting that I came in and shut the door.

'All right,' I said to no one in particular. 'All *right*.' I went in as requested. I went up the stairs and she put her arms round me. 'Did he hurt you?'

'The bastard's got my car.' I don't think at that moment I really believed it. 'I just *stood* there while he got in and drove away.'

'Just as well,' Laurie observed at the top of the stairs. 'He was all set to kill you.'

'I think so. He was strong,' I said. The adrenalin was running down and I suddenly felt tired. 'Thanks for the flowerpot. It could have turned the tide.'

'You should have let me phone.'

'I'll do it now.' I went across the room and poured myself a drink before lifting the receiver and doing the necessary. At that time of night I had confidence that one of the mobiles would spot an easily identifiable car quick enough. Whether they'd catch it was another matter.

I said, 'Keep clear of road blocks, if you can. I don't want him barging his way through.' Not at seven hundred pounds a bumper, I didn't.

The bod at the other end said, 'I'll broadcast to that effect.'

I put the phone down. Laurie said, 'I loved Kitty Chelson. Super.'

'She was terrifying.' The whisky was helping. *A desk job from now on.* Well, on the strength of tonight's performance, not far out. What was the point of weighing a hardish twelve stone when, given a couple of free shots, you can't even make your man cough? Lady Chelson *had* been terrifying. So had Ginger. The only one who hadn't frightened anybody had been yours truly. I said, 'Did you see that cannon Charlie Brown was flourishing? Do you suppose the idiot meant to use it?'

There was a smart tap on the door. Laurie sighed. 'That'll be Peanuts now. You'd better ask him.' She didn't call Sir Charles Peanuts to his face but I suspected he'd have been delighted if she had.

Laurie was right, as usual. Charlie was standing there in a watered silk Hermès dressing-gown which just showed the collar of the lemon yellow silk pyjamas underneath. Presumably he'd been fast asleep when the fun started, but his dark, slightly greying hair was immaculate and I could have sworn he was freshly shaved.

'Just thought I'd make sure we were all right. *You* were all right.' Charlie's English was so colloquially flawless that his apparent inability to sort out his pronouns was rather endearing, although sometimes I thought he did it on purpose.

'No harm done,' I assured him. 'Just strengthening myself with a drink. You'd better have one too.'

'How kind.' Charlie came in and accepted a brandy, padding across the carpet as soundlessly as a cat. Like most Hungarians, he came supplied with Hollywood-style good looks, limitless charm and an ability to wheel and deal. However, unlike many of his countrymen, he never allowed himself to be diverted on his way to the bank. According to his own uninhibited account, Charlie had arrived in England at the age of twenty, penniless and unknown. His first act had been to change his own, somewhat exotic Magyar name to that of the most popular cartoon character he could find. His reasoning: if a nation could love one Charlie Brown, it could love two. The Plantagenet he had added as a kind of aristocratic afterthought. 'Being in the right family still counts in Britain.'

'You'll think he's a clown,' Laurie had told me prior to our first meeting. 'But he's not.'

No clown, Charlie. My word, no. He had worked his way up the income scale by way of ticket-touting, car hire, fast food, package holidays, television and, finally, publishing. Immensely rich, he subsidised sports centres, the arts and, latterly, Third World charities, and on the way he'd acquired British nationality, a handsome and sensible wife called Alice, two presentable sons and a knighthood. The London cottage was one of several homes, all highly attractive, none a vulgar showpiece for his enormous wealth. Some people found his instinctive knack for making money out of virtually anything was slightly off-putting, but so far as I was concerned, not so.

'A little profit here, dear boy, a little there. It all adds up,' Charlie would say as he mentally assessed the chances of recycling the chop bone on his plate. He affected the kind of speech that made him sound rather precious, if not actually gay, but the one hopeful young beauty who tried his luck had found himself abused savagely in Hungarian before being thrown down two flights of stairs.

'We have a name for people like that in Hungary,' Charlie had muttered darkly.

'So have we,' I told him, 'only we're not supposed to use it any more.'

The fact that this oddball was my publisher was simply chance—the result of a takeover bid for an old-established but not very clever firm. God knows, an unbroken diet of Sir Charlie Brown would have been a bit much but, as neighbours, we got on fine.

Now, sipping his drink, Charlie prowled round the room doing his chat bit. 'One cannot leave anything about these days without some dreadful fellow stealing it or blowing it up. If it is important to own an ostentatious car, my dear Angus, *you must put it in a garage.* If you don't, you'll probably find your insurance company won't cough up when expensive things happen to it. You really should read the small print. *I* always do.'

'I bet you do,' I said.

'And why not, pray?' He paused by the desk and peered

at a page of manuscript. 'Who do you sell your old manuscripts to?'

'I don't sell them to anybody,' I said. 'Once the book's printed, I chuck the typescript in the bin.'

Charlie winced. 'You're throwing money away. American universities pay huge sums.'

'Not for my sort of stuff,' I told him. 'But thanks for the Seventh Cavalry act just now. When you waved that cannon of yours at him he was getting ready to eat me alive.'

'The least I could do.'

'What is it, anyway?' Even in the street lighting the weapon had appeared to have about a half-inch bore.

Charlie said with a certain satisfaction, 'It's a Sharpe's buffalo rifle. Eighteen-sixty-two. Highly collectable.'

God, it really was a half-inch bore. 'Does the thing still fire?'

'Of course it fires.'

My ear was cocked for the sound of police sirens. Had they found my car yet?

I said, 'It would blow a hole in a house. Do you happen to have a licence for it?'

Charlie grinned engagingly. 'I'm glad to see we're— you're never off duty. And yes, I have got a licence.'

Well, of course he would have, and I changed the subject a bit guiltily. 'You're right about the car. It was asking for trouble leaving it outside. Now if I'm not lucky it'll end up being quickly shipped to Europe.'

'These days it's more likely to end up being quickly shipped to Africa.'

I thought that was doubtful but didn't want to show my ignorance, so I was glad when Laurie said, 'Why on earth would it go to Africa?'

'Because someone there would buy it, my dear. No questions asked.'

I said, 'Well, they'd have to be out of their minds. Maserati's aren't built for the bush.'

'Maybe not,' Charlie agreed, 'but they make great status symbols. Ask any of your friends who know about African politics—' He broke off. He didn't like to miss anything, Charlie. 'I assume that you have some.'

'Very few.' I felt vaguely put out that he should have tried to pump me on the subject, but then, that sort of thing was Charlie Brown's stock in trade. I said, truly, 'I don't know much about Africa.'

'You should,' Charlie said, 'you should. Ask your friends there about the car trade.' Charlie wasn't a man to push unduly. He glanced at Laurie's carriage clock, ticking away merrily by the window. 'I must go. Alice will think I've been mugged. Thank you both for the drink.'

We watched him cross the mews, not looking in the least bit odd in the Hermès dressing-gown, then locked up for the second time that night.

I finished my drink and brooded about the car. I'd invested the profits of my first, flukily successful novel on a Maserati and stuck to the same make ever since. The thing was an extravagance, a money-consuming toy, but few things had ever given me such genuine pleasure. Just to lift the bonnet and look down on those four overhead camshafts and that great lump of steel and alloy gave me the same kind of æsthetic satisfaction that some people got from studying a Matisse or a Renoir. And at this moment the obscene Ginger was sitting behind that big wood-rimmed wheel going . . . where?

Laurie said, 'I'm going to bed. Are you carrying on working?' Unconsciously she pulled the towelling robe tighter. There was no doubt the thing did something for her. There were, after all, other things in life besides cars.

'It's late,' I agreed. 'Not worth starting work again now.'

The phone rang.

'Yes?'

'Inspector Straun?'

I said, 'Yes, Sergeant Rayner, this is Straun speaking. Any news of my car?'

'One of the mobiles found it, sir. The driver got away.'

'Where was this?'

'Junction of Goldhawk Lane and Linden Grove, sir.'

'And the car?' It was a job making my voice sound normal, but I managed somehow.

Pause.

'Well?'

'Drove it straight into a builder's skip, sir. Didn't do it no good at all.'

CHAPTER 2

Nobody likes to feel a fool and, come morning, I was uncomfortably aware that I hadn't been too clever about Ginger. Perhaps the exigencies of the small hours never look so good in the light of day; even so, the complete police officer should be capable of keeping the peace without the back-up of flowerpot-throwing women. Well, one flowerpot-throwing woman. I should have been grateful, and damn it, I *was* grateful, but I'd have been a good deal happier if I'd done my own fighting. Well, you did do your own fighting, said my conscience, and a lousy job you made of it, losing your car into the bargain. Regrets. Regrets.

I hadn't even nerved myself to inspect the pieces, it being bad enough just telling my garage to go along and sweep them up. Accordingly, I read the morning paper sufficiently intently to preclude conversation and set off on time to earn my daily bread. By ten to nine I was pushing through the glass doors that separated AB Department (Operational Support) from the rest of the third floor of Tiverton House and another day had started. And nothing wrong with a fresh start. At least nobody knew my secret shame.

''Morning, sir,' said Sergeant Endicott. 'Sorry to hear you had a bit of trouble last night.'

I went over to the window and looked out. Down below in Bacton Street, W1 a drizzle of late October rain was beginning to darken the pavements, and a taxi, sensing that the weather was in its favour, lured a fare into the centre of the road before accelerating away and leaving him flat. London. Why hadn't I stayed on in the country, I wondered? Plenty of golf and not a taxi in sight. Because I'd wanted a bit more excitement, I supposed. Because I wanted to be nearer Laurie.

I said sourly, 'News gets around.'

'I'm genuinely sorry, sir. It was a hell of a nice car.' Sergeant Endicott paused discreetly. 'The Chief Superintendent would like a word with you, sir.'

'About this?'

'He didn't say.'

Well, no, he wouldn't, would he? Chief Superintendent Gareth Evans had his pecking order right, and shopping me to my sergeant would have been bad for discipline, supposing Joe Endicott was made that way, which he wasn't. But none of this was the way I'd planned to start my day. Perhaps Laurie was right after all and this was where I started writing whole time for a living. I straightened my tie and headed for my master's door.

'Come.'

I came. Strange how off-putting the omission of the word 'in' could be, a point not missed by Evans the police, a rugby-playing hard man from Pontypridd, black-haired, black-browed and devious as only the Welsh know how.

'What's this they're telling me about drunken goings-on?' Gareth Evans could be Chapel too, when it suited.

I said, 'Nobody was drunk, Chief Superintendent.'

'So what happened?'

I told him what happened, omitting the bit about the flowerpot. I added, 'The car's repairable, with any luck.'

'It'll do the No Claims Bonus no good whatever.'

'No, sir,' I agreed. 'No good whatever.'

Gareth Evans scratched his chin reflectively. Finally he said, 'I'm loaning you to Special Branch. Take your mind off your sorrows.'

'To Special Branch?' I knew he was savouring every moment but it couldn't be helped, because 9.30 a.m. was too early to ride these little surprises.

'You heard.' The Welsh wonder was not exactly rubbing his hands but he didn't look as though he was about to burst into tears either.

'Any particular reason?' Special Branch specialized in the discreet escorting of the great. Special Branch operatives were fit young men who merged with the wallpaper and cultivated a most un-British knack with hand guns. Special Branch did not as a rule recruit late thirty-year-old Inspectors with semi-functioning right shoulders.

Gareth Evans shrugged his full back's shoulders. 'If there is, nobody is telling it to me. Do what you're told, boyo, and hope for the best. Report to Chief Superintendent right away.'

Chief Superintendent Hugget was as small as Gareth Evans was large, close-cropped hair and the sad eyes of a Basset hound. He studied me with what seemed more an air of reproach than anything else. 'I don't imagine you have any experience of escort work?'

I said, 'No, sir. None at all.'

'Last small-arms firing?'

'October last year, sir.'

He fiddled with my personal file as though he was afraid to open it. 'You'd better spend an afternoon on the range with our man before you take up your duties.'

Just a parcel, passed from hand to hand. Aloud I said, 'Very well, sir. But what are my duties?'

'You'll have to ask the Foreign Office about that. Nothing to do with me.' Hugget's red-rimmed eyes grew, if anything, more canine. 'They *asked* for you, Straun. Did you know that? They asked for you *by name*.' He thought that over, something that seemed even worse the second time around. 'I told them you were unsuitable.'

There seemed little to add to that so I shut up. Besides, I could see his point. Hugget presumably spent a lot of time and care training his watchdogs and it must have been galling in the extreme to have their services turned down in favour of an unskilled outsider.

He tossed a card to me across his desk. 'That's the fellow you'll be working for. Todhunter. Take your orders directly from him and try not to make a fool of yourself.' He eyed me curiously. 'Ever heard of the fellow?'

'Our paths crossed on one occasion.'

'Did they now? *Did* they?' Hugget contrived to look as though his worst fears were realized. 'Well, you know what you've let yourself in for, then. Oh yes, you report to him at one o'clock today. East India and Sports. Know where it is?'

By their clubs shall ye know them. Or not, as the case might be. Certainly my brief acquaintanceship with Adrian Todhunter hadn't built up a picture of that particular setting. 'Yes,' I said, 'I know where it is. Do you suppose he's going to buy me lunch?'

'He didn't confide in me.' Hugget paused. I got the feeling that he had a marginally better side and it was telling him that all this wasn't my fault. Finally he said, 'Special Branch isn't a holiday and it's specialized. I tried to make this fellow Todhunter see that, but I very much doubt if I succeeded. Technically, you're his responsibility from now on. But if things get really out of hand you'd better let me know. It's most unlikely I'll be able to do anything about it, but you can always try.'

'I hope it won't come to that,' I said. 'But thanks all the same.'

I cleared things up a little and bade farewell to Sergeant Endicott, who looked suitably impressed.

'You're not going to need a sergeant, by any chance?'

I said, 'If I do, I'll let you know.' I meant it. Joe Endicott was beyond rubies and I didn't want some other pushy Inspector to nick him while I was away, but I could hardly tell him that, so I wished him well and went out to meet Adrian Todhunter.

The East India and Sports sits unobtrusively in one of the corners of St James's Square, a solid, Victorian edifice that once gave comfort to pukka sahibs on the retired list, now presumably to whoever had taken their place. Nabobs of Threadneedle Street? Middling to elderly gents in well-cut city suits went by me as I paused with the porter. Mr Todhunter awaited me in the library. I went on in.

'Good to see you again, Inspector. Glad you could make it.' It was no more than six months since I'd last seen him so I could hardly have expected Adrian Todhunter to age. Same freshly Trumpered hair, same pink, well-scrubbed face. Different suit though, blue-striped. Well-polished shoes and an MCC tie. Eyes bright and alert as a squirrel's.

'Orders,' I said, 'is orders.'

'Well, yes.' We drank sherry, chatted inanities, then went in to lunch.

'Look,' I said, 'I didn't have the chance to say so before but I'm sorry about Jager.' Dirk Jager had been a kind of commercial protégé of the Foreign Office. Unfortunately he had also been a murderer and had come to a bad end, for which I had been responsible. I hadn't had a chance to sound Todhunter out about his feelings until now.

'Water under the bridge.' He caught the steward's eye. 'I'm having smoked salmon and steak and oyster pie. All right for you?'

I said, 'Once in a while.' Then when the man had gone away, 'So what's wrong with the rest of Special Branch that you've got to have me?'

'I need a bodyguard for a VIP.'

Well, I'd guessed something of the sort was coming but being right didn't make it any more attractive. I said, 'Special Branch is crawling with gunfighters.'

'I don't want a gunfighter, as you so quaintly put it.'
Todhunter's school would have knocked the stuffing out of
him but it was a close run thing. He ground peppercorns
over thin, moist slices of smoked salmon. 'I want someone
who knows about golf.'

In their recreational moments the British royal family
seldom sought life beyond the horse, and President Eisenhower had long been a member of the great clubhouse in the
sky. Which left me guarding who? 'There must be plenty of
Special Branch people who play a good game,' I said. 'I
could ask around.'

Todhunter frowned. 'I didn't say I wanted a Sunday-
morning 20 handicapper. I said I wanted someone who
knew about golf. The whole—er—scene.'

The smoked salmon was good but I wasn't in the mood
to enjoy it. 'All right,' I gave up. 'Why?'

'Have you ever heard of a chap called Augustus Aligar?'

'I knew a ghillie once called Augustus,' I said. 'Best I
can do.'

'Of course he's not a ghillie. He's African.'

'African!'

Todhunter winced. 'For God's sake, Angus, try to keep
your voice down. One's fairly safe in assuming the East
India's not bugged but one doesn't have to shout one's
business from the housetops.'

'An African?' I repeated, *diminuendo*.

'Well, I can assure you he doesn't come from County
Meath.' Todhunter paused while the plates were changed.
'He's President of Chakra, as a matter of fact. Any
objections?'

I said, 'It's practically a capital offence to object to anyone on grounds of race, as well you know. Murder your
grandmother and you'll probably get a suspended sentence.
Say you're less than fond of Azerbaijanis and they'll cut
your hands off.' Well, it was Todhunter's lunch after all

and he didn't make our bloody silly laws. 'No, I have no objections to African heads of state. Never met one, if it comes to that. Why does one want to meet me?' Then the penny dropped. 'You mean—?'

'I do indeed,' Todhunter said. 'He's mad about golf. So, as you have presumably just realized, you will serve a dual purpose.'

I thought grimly that very little good came of dual purpose set-ups, which usually ended with nothing working. 'I'm surprised that his own security people wore it,' I said.

'Frankly, so am I,' Todhunter agreed. 'But apparently Aligar absolutely refused to have the usual squad of heavies following him around, which incidentally gives some idea of the clout the man carries. We, of course, had to insist on providing some sort of cover—it would be an impossible situation if some maniac decided to murder him while he was over here.'

'And he accepted that?'

Todhunter sniffed. 'He created a certain amount of fuss, but of course he saw our point. But he insisted we provided someone he'd fine congenial and able to fulfil his special requirements.' He paused. 'And so, Angus, I naturally thought of you.'

I said, 'That's very nice of you, Adrian.' I wondered who had really put my name forward, but not for long, because the answer stuck out a mile. Charlie Plantagenet Brown would enjoy furthering my career. Even more, he'd like knowing exactly the right man in the right department. And most of all, he'd delight in getting half Whitehall jumping before breakfast. Just the same, I wish he'd asked me first. 'What,' I asked, 'is he like as a chap?'

Todhunter allowed himself a smile. 'I can assure you he's not a tribal muscle man or an over-ambitious army officer. He's bright, American-educated, no hang-ups—and very

good company. You could say that for once a country's got
the right man at the right time.'

I'd heard Foreign Office officials say the same before and
get it wrong, so I asked, 'In what way?'

Todhunter ignored the question by asking one of his own.
'How much do you know about Chakra?'

'Frankly,' I told him, 'not much. Apart from the fact that
it's in Africa. But I can always get a guide book from the
library.'

Todhunter said, 'That I seriously doubt, since it's hardly
been heading the popularity stakes for package holidays,
but you can try. Up till now the place has been run incredibly badly by Aligar's uncle, who finally went too far and
got himself killed in the kind of road accident that one
doesn't go into too thoroughly. Augustus Aligar's been living the life of an exile up till now—mainly in the United
States. He's been called back by what's generally called
"popular demand" and by all accounts he's going to take
the job seriously. We're more than happy to welcome him
here.'

'Would it be tactless to ask why?'

'Commercial considerations,' Todhunter added, rather
hurriedly I thought, 'but he really is a most delightful chap.
And he's truly potty about golf. He seems to have taken to
it fairly late in life—he's forty-five, by the way—and he
seems anxious to make up for lost time.' Todhunter added,
'As a player, I gather he's not particularly good, but they
tell me he's building the country's first golf course with
an eye to the tourist trade. A forward thinking character.
However, there is just one other thing—'

Todhunter did not look furtive but he would have done
had he known the meaning of the word. 'President Aligar
comes complete with friend. Very attractive, I'm told.'

'I'm happy for him,' I said. 'Male or female?'

Todhunter looked pained. 'A young woman, of course.

Her name is Kiki Bouchier. An American citizen, coloured.
A lady golfer of renown, I gather. Now I understand you
have a friend who plays golf. Miss Wilson? It would be
convenient if the four of you—'

'Oh no,' I said.

'Miss Wilson's not a golfer?'

I said, 'Oh no, I'm not providing that kind of foursome.'
I felt coldly angry, and why not? Policemen are public
servants, but up to a point their private lives are supposed
to be their own. Todhunter, damn him, or that little creep
Gareth Evans had been pawing over mine and come up
with this highly convenient morsel. I could hear him milling
it over.

*'Sleeping with this woman, Straun is, and neither been inside
chapel in their lives! Sinful it is, but useful. No reputation to lose,
see?'*

'Well, it's nothing to get on your high horse about,' Todhunter told me. 'I should think Miss Wilson might find the
whole thing rather amusing.'

'Well, I don't intend to ask her.'

'Don't be a fool, Angus. Huffing and puffing will get you
nowhere.' Todhunter topped up my glass. 'Besides, you
understand perfectly well that business is business.'

I drank some of the wine while I calmed myself down,
anger being an expensive luxury, and in any case I was
more critical of myself than anyone else. A bit old to be
surprised by life's quaint paradoxes. Cuckolded husbands
have always been figures of fun, the righteously indignant
invariably ridiculous. 'Tell me,' I asked with genuine
curiosity, 'what would you have suggested if I'd been
married?'

Todhunter looked blank. 'My dear fellow, I haven't the
faintest idea. But you're not, are you?'

Losing tempers gets one nowhere. 'Listen, Adrian,' I
said, 'if my masters wish to sell me to you chaps in the

Foreign Office, there's very little I can do about it. But if any friend of mine chooses to tell you to go to hell, that's it.'

'You have a gift for doing things the hard way, don't you?' Todhunter said. 'And we're not talking about your "friends", we're discussing Miss Wilson. All we ask is that occasionally when you're out and about with our visitors she should join the party. Were you married it would be different because a wife is instinctively antagonistic towards a mistress and we'd never achieve a happy foursome that way. But two couples in what we can loosely describe as a similar situation—well, it's all very relaxed, isn't it? And relaxed is what we want Aligar's visit to be. He's got to feel *accepted*.'

'And just supposing Miss Wilson doesn't wish to be relaxed with your happy pair?' I asked.

Todhunter stared out of the window at his side, a pointless thing to do, the view being minimal. He said, 'How do the Americans put it? *You can't beat City Hall.* You know as well as I do that pressure can be brought to bear.'

I said, 'Don't talk balls. The Foreign Office may be my master but it's certainly not hers. What would you use as a big stick?' But I asked without conviction because everyone is a hostage to something or other.

Todhunter waggled his hand. 'Oh, I expect we'd find something. She goes to New York on business quite frequently, I understand. It would be annoying if she started to have trouble over her American visa.'

He could do it, I realized. Even if there wasn't some unholy alliance between Todhunter and his counterpart in Grosvenor Square, there was always the law to fall back on. Something such as a well-set-up case of soliciting would fix any girl's chances of getting into the land of the free.

'Remind me,' I said, 'to do something for you, sometime.'

Todhunter nodded. 'I know, dear boy. But we have been

asked to keep Mr Aligar happy, and keep him happy we shall. For that we need both you and your friend. End of discussion.'

'Yes,' I agreed, 'you make it admirably clear.' I had no foolish notions that these were empty threats. The Todhunters of this world play for real, and he hadn't forgiven me for the fate of an earlier protégé who had asked for trouble and got it in a big way. 'So if I'm to entertain Mr Aligar, you'd better give me a list of things he wants me to do.'

Todhunter smiled placidly. 'Oh, I'm sure he'll do that for himself. He had a luncheon he couldn't avoid today but he promised to join us for coffee.'

'He'll be late.'

Wrong again. President Augustus Aligar made his entry exactly on cue, not unlike the Demon King. He was short, thick-set, and very dark, with an elegant, almost fragile bone structure that looked more Arab than Negro. He wore the kind of tight black beard favoured by the Mogul emperors, through which his teeth showed the usual dazzling white. The blue chalk-stripe suit looked to me like Savile Row, the button-down shirt was undoubtedly Brooks Brothers and whoever had built the presidential shoes would have been pleased to see that they were clean and highly polished. He looked younger than his reputed age of forty-five and, apart from general good looks, the man positively radiated energy as he bounced towards our table.

'Hi there!'

I don't know what I'd expected him to sound like but not like your friendly neighbourhood New York cab-driver.

'Hi!' I said. Ever the cosmopolitan.

'Good morning, Mr President.' Todhunter was a Foreign Office official and not for anybody was he going to be anything else. He stood up and shook hands, though. 'May I present Inspector Straun—'

'Great! Heard a lot about you, Inspector.' A huge, hairy hand seized mine and squashed it. 'Look, call me, Gus, OK? Going to see quite a bit of each other so start as you mean to go on, I always say.' He sank into a chair and motioned to the waiter to pour him some coffee. 'Hell, but it's all go.'

I listened with the kind of fascination I hoped wasn't showing on my face. Where had he learned his curiously dated American that even to me, no expert, sounded like the soundtrack of an old film?

I made appropriate noises. Strange now ineffectual one can be when the unexpected is dumped on your lap. What had I imagined this man was going to be like, anyway? A stage Othello? Well, that he wasn't, but I told myself there was no actual law against someone using a Brooklyn cab-driver as a linguistic coach. I also told myself that, odd though he might sound, there was no getting away from the fact that Augustus Aligar's English was at least fluent and understandable, which was more than could be said for my Soshi.

'Todhunter here tell you about the golf bit? That you gotta know how to play?'

'Yes,' I said. 'He told me.'

His big dark eyes studied me over the coffee cup. 'Great. So what d'ya play to?'

I said, 'My handicap's six. What's yours?'

I thought Todhunter winced a bit, but who'd started all this anyway?

'Four,' Gus said. Then, rather more firmly, 'Four!'

All right, so he was four. I wondered whether to ask where but then changed my mind. Instead I said, 'I'm afraid I'm not very clear what it is you want me to do. Apart from guarding your person.'

'Guarding my person!' Gus beamed appreciatively. 'Guarding my person! I like that. Kind of British understatement.'

I said, 'We're renowned for it. But what else do you want
me to do?'

He put his coffee cup down carefully, as though afraid
he might break it. 'You know how many golf courses we
got in Chakra?'

I said, 'One, still not completed.' The President looked
pleased. 'You're dead right. Courses ready, none.' He considered. 'That's all going to change.'

'There are big plans to develop the area for high-class
international tourism,' Todhunter informed me briskly. He
gave the impression that he'd thought up the idea himself.

'Sure, that's right.' Gus didn't look any too pleased about
the story being taken away from him but was too nice to
do much about it.

'That's where golf comes in.' Todhunter put his fingertips
together and made a little house. 'Everyone expects golf
these days.' He made it sound as though the game was a
passing fancy, like wind-surfing.

So I wasn't to be bodyguard to just one more golf addict,
I was to look after a Head of State kind of Minister for Golf.
I sat and thought it over.

African golf has always been centred round the great
colonial courses. Third World golf as a means of attracting
tourist money seemed just as viable as game parks without
having to worry about poachers. I looked at Aligar. 'How
many courses do you plan on having?'

I think if he'd said twenty I'd have back-pedalled somehow or other, but he wasn't letting his own enthusiasm run
away with him. He held up a long, well-manicured index
finger. 'Like I said, I got me one to start with, at Kinto.
Just about ready to go.'

'Who designed it?'

'British outfit. Panorama Golf Construction.'

I nodded. They were a well-established firm, any course
they built would be at least adequate. 'And after that?'

The President made a 'who knows?' waggle with his hands. 'Me, I'd say you can't have too much of a good thing. But maybe we try this one first and see how we get on?'

I said, 'Very sensible.'

'But while I'm here—'

Out of the corner of my eye I could see Todhunter looking at me. All right. All right. 'While you're here,' I said on cue, 'you'd like to play a little golf.'

Aligar nodded, a bit impatiently I thought. 'Sure, that'll be great. But I'd like to look around a few clubs, if that's OK with you.'

'I'm sure there'll be no difficulty about that.' Todhunter, smoothly reassuring.

Aligar ignored him. 'I don't want to build some kind of glitz clubhouse folk are going to laugh at. You show me the odd top of the pile clubhouse, then I'll know what I'm after.'

'Very sensible,' I told him. His readiness to learn was obviously genuine, and I wondered how such an enthusiast for the game managed to know so little about the traditional 19th hole. I'd have asked, but Todhunter wouldn't have liked it.

Aligar was smiling with relief. 'There you go, then. You reckon I could get to meet a secretary or two?'

'Nothing easier,' I told him. 'No problem.'

'Great. Now, how about me buying you gentlemen a brandy?'

I watched Todhunter wince. How does one break the news tactfully to a distinguished Head of State that guests don't order drinks in their host's club? Maybe they did in Kinto. What would the elegant Todhunter say? Mercifully nothing awful. 'My dear fellow, let me—'

'Did you play much golf in the States, Mr President?' Have you read any good books lately? Well, I had to say something while the steward came up.

'Gus. Call me Gus.' Intentionally or not, Aligar ignored my question. 'They got some fine courses over there. Say, you know where's the lowest golf club in the world?'

The lowest. It rang some sort of anecdotal bell. Maybe we weren't still talking about America. 'Isn't there one somewhere near the Dead Sea?'

'Say, you're not bad!' Gus's face lit up with appreciation. 'The Sodom and Gomorrah at Kallia—1,250 feet below sea level. Only it burnt down—the clubhouse, I mean. Maybe they don't use it any more.'

'Must have been fire and brimstone,' Todhunter said, keeping his end up. He didn't play golf but he knew his Old Testament all right.

Gus looked puzzled. 'The way I heard it, it was some kind of fire in the kitchen.'

There was a discreet pause, while brandy was doled out. All knowledge is useful, so I registered the fact that President Aligar was weak on R.I. but strong on *The Guinness Book of Records*. I said, 'So I introduce you to some club secretaries. Anything else?'

'Maybe a look at catering? Costs per head and profit margins? That kind of thing? General course overheads, ground staff. How much you get to write down your equipment against tax. What you pay your agronomists.' Gus thought that little lot over. 'Can do?'

'We'll work something out,' I assured him. It looked as though he wasn't going to be the only one to widen his knowledge.

'One more thing.'

'Yes?'

'I'd sure as hell like to play a round at The Rogues.'

CHAPTER 3

The Rogues. Well, it was hardly a municipal course. I had a course guide at home that listed it rather tersely:

Founded 1934 by Ernest Clarkson, course designed by William Broad. Membership: closed. Facilities: n/a. Green fees: closed to non-members. Address: Thornton Basset, Norfolk. Telephone: Ex-Dir. 18 holes. 6972 yards. Professional: Not listed.

I knew a bit more, but not much more than the legendary bits. I knew that 'Uncle Ernie' Clarkson had been a millionaire bookmaker who was reputed to have been blackballed by Wentworth and had retaliated by constructing a fabulous course in East Anglia with a membership open only to characters as dubious as himself. I knew that to be a Rogue a love of golf was essential, but, apart from that, it had been every man for himself. In Uncle Ernie's day applicants had been hand-vetted. Their money had to have been ill-gotten, their reputations deplorable and a prison record almost guaranteed acceptance. But they enjoyed the facilities of what was possibly the finest 18 holes in Europe and beyond question the most exclusive. Tournament players, politicians and golfing royals were *personae non grata* by virtue of office, but others who sought out members and angled for a single round were rarely successful. The Rogues didn't want guests. They'd been outcasts of society too long for it to be important to them, and for years they played happily among themselves.

Latterly they were reputed to have become less gamey, and a few members were said to lead comparatively lawful lives, but they were still a rum old lot who guarded their privacy with fanatical zeal. Well-informed rumour had it that members were allowed two guests each per year, a privilege for which the host paid two hundred pounds a round. There was also a list of clubs—Wentworth heading the list—whose members were not admitted under any circumstances, on the grounds that Rogues, like elephants, never forgot. There might equally well have been a list of unacceptable visitors; if so, one might imagine that all members of Her Majesty's police forces would be inscribed thereon in letters of fire.

'I wouldn't know how to go about getting myself a round at The Rogues,' I informed Todhunter as soon as we were alone. 'How in God's name do you suppose I can fix it for four of us? You're dealing with people who go out of their way to be bloody-minded. If the Secretary of the R and A wanted a game I don't suppose he'd get it.'

Todhunter said mildly, 'Aligar's black, isn't he? Threaten the bastards with the Race Relations Act.'

'From what I've seen of Aligar,' I told him, 'he wouldn't take kindly to being patronized by that bit of legal hogwash. Quite apart from the fact that the Rogues wouldn't have Eisenhower, donkey's years ago. If the Rogues can say no to the President of the United States, I don't imagine the head boy of Chakra has much of a chance. Precedent is precedent.'

Todhunter sighed. 'Really, Angus, there are times when I think you like making difficulties. Just find a way, there's a good chap. After all, it's your sport, not mine.'

He was right, too. I went over everything I knew about the Rogues, *everyone* I knew. Not many. Sid Walker?

Well, nobody does anything for a copper for nothing. Very few people, in my experience, do anything for *anybody* unless they have their reasons, and in any case a policeman's lot is hard enough without putting himself under obligation. Just the same, I needed Sid Walker's help, so I asked him to join me in a drink.

'Very kind of you, I'm sure, Mr Straun. Just across the road at twelve do you?'

Just across the road would be the Cross Keys in Avery Street, a stone's throw from Walker's Sale Rooms, where suits of plate, crossbows, carronade balls, and suchlike militaria of former times regularly came under the hammer for prices that would make you blink. Sid Walker and his brother Geoff were the unlikely but immensely knowledgeable pair who jointly owned the firm, although to look at them you'd imagine that a barrow in the Old Kent Road would have suited them best. For all I'd ever found out, it may have done at one time. But not now.

I got to the Cross Keys on time, but Sid was there before me. His dark grey suit looked as though it might well have come from the same tailor favoured by Gus Aligar, and I guessed that shoes, shirt and so on were equally well bred, but the Walkers looked ill at ease in clothes in the way that boxers do, big men with big muscles in the wrong places. Had they been fighters in some previous life? Something had broken Sid's nose, but he could have done that falling over in church. Whatever it was, it hadn't softened his brain. Bright as a button was Sid.

''Morning, Mr Straun.' He stood up in the old-fashioned oak booth and ushered me in.

''Morning, Mr Walker.' It was the sort of occasion that calls for given names but I didn't wish to presume. After all, our association was—apart from the odd divergent occasion—strictly business. I enjoyed collecting odd pieces of mediæval weaponry, Sid Walker presumably enjoyed selling them to me. Still, I'd done the odd thing for him in the past, so you could say he owed me. But how much?

'What'll it be?'

Sid was drinking something pale brown that looked like Scotch but could well have been ginger ale, lunch-time drinking not being favoured by the serious business classes.

But I ordered whisky and we drank to each other as though this was something we did every day.

'And very agreeable, too.' Sid put his glass down and studied me benignly. This meeting hadn't been his idea, so he wasn't worrying. He asked courteously, 'Been having a few rounds lately, have we?'

The natural reaction of a gentleman. Neither his business nor mine to set the ball rolling. I felt badly about ignoring the offer but I had no desire to be in the Cross Keys all afternoon. I said, 'Look, for my sins I've been landed with the job of playing nursemaid to a golf-mad African politician. Not only that, but I'm expected to fix him up with a game at The Rogues.'

'Are you now?' Sid looked pained. 'Could be difficult, that—very.'

I said, 'As it happened, I was going to ask if you could help.'

Sid blew on his nails and gave them a polish on his sleeve. He had a hand like a Sunday joint. He looked up at me. 'Funny old lot at The Rogues, so I hear. What makes you so sure I'm a member?'

'Well, aren't you?' Which was a bit brutal but Sid wasn't built for pussyfooting about.

Sid swallowed some more of whatever it was he was drinking. 'Too right I am, though it ain't exactly public knowledge.'

'Someone leaked a list of members.' They hadn't. Anyone leaking anything from The Rogues would have risked ending up in a dark alley with two broken legs. On the other hand I could hardly explain that a couple of years back I'd had the Walker brothers checked out by the Fraud people, who are good at that sort of thing as a rule. With Sid they had got about as far as his golf club and not much else, but I could hardly tell him that.

'Bloody 'ell,' Sid said without visible surprise. 'You can't

trust nobody these days.' He added, 'I did hear you 'ave
an open invitation, though.'

I was genuinely moved. 'Thanks, Mr Walker. It's very
good of you.'

Sid sighed. 'On my mother's grave, Mr Straun, it's nothing to do with me.'

'Not your invitation?'

'Not mine, so help me.' Sid caught someone's eye and
our glasses were refilled and I paid. It *was* ginger ale he
was drinking. He swirled the stuff round in his glass, rather
as though expecting it to turn to wine. 'Not that I wouldn't
have been glad to oblige, 'ad I known.'

'I appreciate that, Mr Walker.' True, too. I was angry
with myself for embarrassing him. Why the devil had I just
assumed it was Sid who'd made The Rogues available?
Why hadn't I checked first? I drank some whisky as I
tried to think rationally. I hadn't checked for the very good
reason that there wasn't any way of checking. And I'd
assumed my sponsor to have been Sid because he happened
to be the only member I knew.

I said, 'If it wasn't you, who was it?'

'Important, is it?' Extraordinary how delicate Sid Walker
could be, the wary-footedness of big men.

'Yes,' I said, 'pretty important.' I corrected myself, 'Well,
it could be important. I don't know.'

Sid looked at me. You don't pick up much from the face
of a professional auctioneer. He could have been feeling
sorry for me, but he could equally well have been wondering
what kind of police force he was paying taxes for. Finally
he said, 'Funny old day, innit?'

'Yes,' I said, 'a funny old day.'

Sid sighed. I think he was almost on the point of asking
to be let off but fair was fair, he probably reckoned I'd
bought the odd thing from him now and then and was a
copper into the bargain. Nobody knows when they might

want the law, a cynical thought, but true. In Sid's business you can have urgent need of the boys in blue almost any time. He said, 'It's just luck really, innit, Mr Straun? I mean, I wouldn't have known anything about it if I hadn't been on the committee.'

The Sid Walkers of this world don't usually sit on golf club committees but then The Rogues was not an ordinary golf club. But even so, I said, 'You mean, before a member can invite a guest he has to ask your committee?'

'He's an overseas member, Mr Straun. Special rules there are for overseas members.'

And members in jail? It wasn't a question one could ask, although hard not to wonder. I'd imagined the Rogues had become rather more staid over the years, but Sid was making me not so sure.

'And this overseas member's name, Mr Walker?'

'Name of O'Shea, Mr Straun. Patrick O'Shea.' Sid paused delicately. 'Known in the trade as Birdie.'

Birdie O'Shea. Well, it took you back. Six, seven years back, in fact. But then if you cast your bread upon the waters it shall come back to you, just as the Good Book says.

'Birdie says—' Sid paused, as though to consider how best to frame it—'as how you did him a good turn.'

'You could put it that way.'

'Like gettin' him started on golf.' Something inexorable about Sid. Like one's dotty aunt who insisted on recounting in detail the plot of a book she knows you've read for yourself. Obviously Sid knew all about the early life of Birdie O'Shea. Equally obvious that he wanted me to tell him all over again. Well, it was hardly confidential.

I said, 'I took some evidence from him when he was on remand in 'eighty-three or -four. It struck me at the time that he'd been unlucky—that the case against him didn't really stand up. I put in a word for him and we were lucky—the bench listened, and he got off.' I remembered him pretty well, as a matter of fact. He must have been in his twenties then, a raw-boned little Lowlander who'd strayed down south and got himself into some kind of trouble. I remember there'd been a Ryder Cup match on at the time and he'd amused me by asking how a couple of the matches were getting on. I'd asked him if he played himself.

'Aye. But not since I came down south.'

He'd told me he used to play at some municipal course I'd never heard of. He'd been a caddie and someone called Major Stewart had given him a half set of cast-off clubs. 'A grand man he was. But he couldna play worth a damn.'

'I asked him what his handicap was,' I told Sid, 'and he told me he was plus 1.'

Sid did his sceptical auctioneer bit. 'If you ask me, Mr Straun, he was havin' you on. Did you believe him?'

'I didn't disbelieve him.' I'd played to scratch myself once upon a long time, a very serious amateur, and I knew that players with a penalty handicap are about as rare as hen's teeth. I said, 'We chatted about golf for quite a while. He'd seen me play that year in the Open and he asked me if I'd give him a game, always supposing that he got off. Which he did.'

Sid emptied his glass and caught the barman's eye. 'An' did you?'

'Yes,' I said, 'we did, as a matter of fact. I remember he beat me three and two.'

'An' you got him a job.'

'There was a club I knew that needed an assistant. I just pointed O'Shea in the right direction.'

Sid looked pleased, as though he'd found out something that had been worrying him. 'He owes you, Mr Straun.' He went so far as to rub his hands. 'Oh yes, he owes you.'

I didn't want Birdie O'Shea to owe me. He'd been a

bright enough young man who'd hopped into trouble and hopped out again, either because the bench of magistrates had behaved sensibly for once or because he'd been dead lucky. All I really knew about Birdie was that he'd been a hell of a good golfer and that whichever club had taken him on must have got a very worthwhile assistant pro. 'I lost touch with him,' I said. 'I thought he might have got somewhere but I never saw his name.'

'Oh, he got somewhere all right,' Sid told me. 'Oh my word, yes. Gave up golf just after you knew 'im. As I 'eard it, Birdie made himself unpopular in certain quarters, an' someone took 'im up a back alley one night and broke 'is arm in three places, which didn't do 'is swing no good at all. So he went into business with another feller who was into the construction lark and between them they went into building golf courses. Mind you,' Sid said judiciously, 'Birdie ain't no Jack Nicklaus, no more's his mate, but from what I 'ear, for the sort of places wot hires them, they're good enough.'

'What kinds of places?' I had a pretty good idea of the answer but it wouldn't have been fair to disappoint Sid.

'Middle East mainly. Lotta prestige golf courses there these days.' He did his best to look casual. 'I 'ear it's Africa now.'

'Panorama Golf Construction,' I said.

I thought it over. Certainly it explained how little Birdie O'Shea had got himself enough clout to get into The Rogues, which I imagined was just his kind of club, and a grateful Birdie would account for his eagerness that the President and I should get our game. I tried to imagine Birdie pulling strings all those miles away like some master-puppeteer, but found it pretty difficult. To be honest, I found it difficult even to remember what the man looked like.

I said, apropos of nothing in particular, 'Why is he called

Birdie anyway?' It wasn't something that worried me, just something to say.

Sid rubbed his nose reflectively. 'Maybe it was because he scored a lot of birdies—you'd have to make a hell of a lot to play better than scratch. Then again it could be because he done bird. Which he 'ad.'

I'd forgotten Birdie O'Shea had had a prison record, if I'd ever known. I said, 'What was he in for?'

'Same as always,' Sid told me cheerfully. 'Nicking cars. Once they start as kids they never seem to stop. Funny, innit?'

CHAPTER 4

Is there a man with a soul so dead that it doesn't at least
stir at the sight of winter sunshine and the knowledge that
he's going to get a round in? I stood at the window while
Laurie was dressing and hoped all would be well, as she
hadn't been overjoyed at the news that Todhunter had
press-ganged her into joining the party.

'You mean,' she'd said, 'that you've been *ordered* to turn
up complete with mistress just to keep this tinpot president
company?'

I'd cursed Todhunter yet again. 'I don't think people
have mistresses these days.'

'Live-in girlfriend? Sleeping partner?'

I'd said, 'I don't imagine he put it so undiplomatically.'

'I'd have said he'd made the idea fairly plain.' No, not
amused. 'As I see it, we're playing a mixed foursomes, each
gentleman to partner whoever he's laying at the moment.'

Christ. 'Yes, since you put it like that.'

Laurie's mouth twitched. 'Your friend Todhunter's really
fixed you, hasn't he.' Not a question, a statement.

I'd said yes, he had.

Pause. Then: 'Well, it all sounds a riot of a weekend. I
can't wait.' Dotty, unpredictable, my girl and none other.

Now, waiting, puzzled but grateful, I wondered if the
night had brought any change, but when she joined me I
saw that mercifully it hadn't because she was dressed for
the day ahead. Some women would have worn clothes that
shrieked golf at a hundred paces, but Laurie was slackless
and checkless, looking as though she was going to spectate
rather than play. She took in my appraising glance.

'All right?'

She was more than all right, as she very well knew. I said, 'You're a credit to the Force.' I gave her a hug but she jumped back as though I'd stuck a knife into her.

'For God's sake, Angus, what's that under your jacket?'

A .38 Smith and Wesson to be exact, in a shoulder-holster just like James Bond. I said, 'Well, I'm supposed to be an escort, after all, and you know as well as I do that Special Branch personnel are armed. It's just routine.'

I thought for a moment that she was going to make a thing of it, but she eventually nodded. 'I suppose so.'

A moment of contrition. 'I'm sorry,' I said, 'I should never have got involved but I didn't have much choice.' But I wondered if that was strictly true. I could have resigned or threatened to expose Adrian Todhunter to the Sunday press or whatever, but I knew I wouldn't have done it and so did she.

'It's not your fault. Just the bloody job.' Most of the time a forceful girl but mercifully not given to sulks, Laurie managed to smile and look as though she meant it. 'Forget it. What time did you say we picked your President up?'

I said, 'He's not my President, thank God. But we meet him at the Embassy at ten.'

'At *ten*?'

'I know,' I said. 'Lots of time. But I'd like to call at the garage on the way down and see what Oscar has to say about the car.' Oscar Louth ran a small Maserati-only service enterprise in a cul-de-sac off the Bayswater Road. Not even in my wildest moments of self-deception would I have called his work cheap but it was done with a care that amounted almost to love. In my book, anyone with a Maserati would have to be mad to go anywhere else. At this moment I wasn't looking forward to seeing what my car looked like after hitting a skip, but it was best to get it over.

Laurie asked, 'Have you called for a taxi?'

I shook my head. Being the kind of person that taxis take care to avoid, I'd laid on a hire car, which was probably just as well as it arrived on time and a couple of suitcases and two sets of golf clubs went into the boot without comment, which would hardly have been the case with one's friendly neighbourhood taxi-driver. Comfortably, we drove west against the morning flood of commuter traffic heading resolutely east. It took longer to reach Cabel Gardens than I'd expected, the kind of thing that tends to presage one of those days. As we arrived at the cul-de-sac I told the driver to wait, and got out. Fingers crossed. Hope for the best.

''Morning, Mr Straun.' A large, blue-overalled character clutching a spotless spoked Boranni wheel in one huge hand.

''Morning, Paddy.' I got out and followed him into the office, so-called. Peregrine Motors had started life in a mews, latterly had moved to Cabel Gardens, a most ungardenlike collection of shanty buildings that must at some time have had something to do with the nearby railway, I had no idea what. These unlikely premises were spotlessly clean and rarely housed less than half a dozen elderly Maseratis in course of repair or restoration, plus a few more that were available for sale. They were mainly high performance road cars, Boras, Ghiblis, Khamsins and the like, owned or about to be owned by one-make fanatics like myself. A few were pure competition cars, prepared and maintained for vintage racing. Nothing would change hands for less than the price of a house, many would fetch quite a nice one. Their owners had brought their playthings to these primitive surroundings because Oscar Louth knew more about Maseratis than anyone else in the country. Peregrine Motors didn't look much but it was the best.

'Oscar said he might have an estimate for my repairs,' I told Paddy. 'Is he around?'

The Irishman shook his head. He was a good fitter but

as a conversationalist he took his time. Finally he got
around to it. 'He said last night he was planning to
take Mr Deacon's car out early to see how she handled.
You know how the gentleman is about his suspension
set-up.'

'I do indeed,' I said. I knew Bill Deacon slightly, an
architect whose car was a twin to mine, a man with an
obsession, who would have had his suspension and steering
rebuilt each week if it resulted in even marginally improved
handling. For a racing driver it would have made sense,
but Bill Deacon was a bit of an old woman behind the
wheel, racked with guilt every time he exceeded the speed
limit by more than a couple of miles an hour. 'Look,' I said,
'have you any idea when he's likely to be back?'

'Any minute, to be sure.'

I looked at my watch. With Paddy, any minute could
well mean any thirty minutes, any hour come to that. Oscar
could well be doing a deal on his way back, or having it off
with the lady next door for all I knew. Like many perfec-
tionists, he could be curiously unpredictable when about
his own affairs.

'I'll give him five minutes,' I said. I suppose I'd have
done better to leave it where it was, but few of us can leave
a sore tooth alone. 'Where's what's left of my car?'

'The far shed. You'll not miss it.'

'It'll only spoil your day,' Laurie said. But she came
along too. I'd been in this late addition to Oscar's premises
once before, and that when it was an empty shell just after
he'd bought it. Now, according to his lights, he'd got it
furnished. I stood and admired. The central stove was no
great shakes, a kind of vast homemade brazier constructed
from king-sized oil drums, but the rest of the gear must
have cost a bomb. I took in a milling machine, a big Myford
lathe and a battery of gas cylinders he'd use for welding.
At least a quarter of the available room was given over to

the, to me, unidentifiable gear used for shaping curved body panels from sheet steel, everything orderly and immaculate, as were the tools that lined the walls. In the far right of the shed was a car. My car.

'Oh Angus!' Laurie was a girl who could normally take cars or leave them alone but the Khamsin was a sight that would have drawn tears from a stone. I walked over and took it in at close range. My strong friend Ginger had managed to hit something just about head on and the front of the car was bent in a kind of large 'V'. The grille had gone, and the headlamps had come round to meet each other, so to speak, or they would have done if they hadn't both been shattered. The impact had concertina'd most of the front body panels, and I had little doubt that the shock would have distorted the back as well. Mechanically, I didn't like to think. The front wheels had the knock-kneed effect that comes when the suspension has completely gone, and although I could have prised open the bonnet and had a look at the engine my courage didn't run to it. Radiator, fan and a good deal of plumbing must have been slammed back over the motor, doing God knows how much damage. I shivered. Cold or not, it wasn't a pretty sight.

Laurie said briskly, 'You'd have done far better to stay away.'

'I suppose so.' I must have looked pretty sick, because she looked at me curiously.

'Darling, are you all right?'

'Yes, of course.' In fact, I wasn't. Art is subjective, after all, and there's always something obscene about vandalism. But I'd experienced that odd, cold touch on my shoulder before. Why does it always seem to be the Scots who have old aunts with the Sight? Mercifully, she hadn't passed on much to me, just enough to make me uncomfortable now and then. A sense of something dark. A feeling that would have made a kind of sense on an ancient field of battle or a ruined dungeon but seemed to have little place among machinery and shining tools. I could feel the palms of my hands dampening with cold sweat. 'Time we were going,' I said.

I told Paddy to let Oscar know I'd called and we got back in the hire car.

The Chakranian Embassy is in a wide, tree-lined road off the southern end of Kensington High Street. There was a time, getting on for a century ago, when wealthy merchants built themselves large, solid houses there, and hid them behind trees and high walls. Now the merchants have gone and the Diplomatic Corps has moved in. Parking is a problem, because the road is full of the big, black limousines whose chauffeurs cheerfully park wherever their fancy dictates, secure in the knowledge that they can tear up their parking tickets because the long-suffering British will honour their diplomatic immunity.

'What number for the Republic of Chakra?' Laurie asked.

'Eight,' I told her.

Eight had a yellow Rolls Corniche convertible parked outside.

'Hi!' President Augustus Aligar waved a large paw at me. He was wearing a lovat mixture jacket over a yellow cashmere sweater. You might look at him but you wouldn't laugh. He nodded down at his vehicle. 'Some car!'

I waved back at him. Some car indeed. There had been a time when there had been many a yellow Rolls-Royce in the choicer streets of London, elegant, coachbuilt things with black wings and the driver sitting out in the open. Yellow, as of now, wasn't exactly in, but Gus's Corniche almost carried it off.

I opened the door for Laurie and we went across to get the introductions over. Gus was not alone.

'We're going to have a wonderful time. Just wonderful!

But first I want you to meet my friend. The name's Kiki. Kiki Bouchier.'

Kiki Bouchier smiled and said, 'Hello there!' Conversationally it may have been no big deal, but then she didn't have to try. Racially, she was either a very pale-skinned Negress or one of the exotic blood mixes one finds around the Mississippi delta. From the way she sat in the car I guessed she was a tall girl. Small face, huge dark eyes and a vivid red mouth. Hair, raven black and dead straight, gathered in the nape of the neck with what looked like a clip of stones that matched her emerald shirt. For all I knew the stones were emerald, too. To judge from her company and quite staggering good looks, they probably were.

'You go with the car,' I said.

She gave a hoot of laughter. 'Watch what you say, man. The car's rented.' A trace of French accent. I remembered vaguely that the Creoles of Louisiana spoke French, or had a French-based patois of their own. Hard to know if I was remembering fact or some Hollywood film, but the voice was deep and dark all right. I could imagine her as a singer if I hadn't known about the girl.

The President said, 'You'd better get in before you say something you'll regret.' He looked as though he was enjoying himself, but so far as I could make out he always looked that way. Of course I hadn't seen him running his country, not usually the happiest of jobs and none of my business anyway.

I saw our gear loaded into the boot of the Corniche, paid off the hire car and we were away. Laurie sat next to sir, I made do with Kiki in the back, a disturbing experience, never having understood about people radiating sex before. We drove out on to the Bayswater Road. I made noises like turning left.

Gus said, 'OK, OK, you sent me a route map. Where do we stay?'

I said, 'We're booked in at the Bell at Hendringham. About five miles from the club.'

'The Bell?' Gus flipping the Corniche through the office-going traffic with the ruthless expertise of the driver schooled in Manhattan but without the latter's fretting about the wrong side of the road.

'It's an inn,' I said. 'Very comfortable. Well known, in fact.' My contribution to British understatement, the Bell being the kind of inn that charges a hundred quid a night, supplies a fourposter bed and jacuzzi to every room and has a three-rosette listing in the good food guides. Not my kind of pub, but then this was not my kind of outing and, with any luck, the taxpayer would be picking up the bill.

Kiki said huskily, 'Me, I never stayed at an inn.'

'You must have led a very sheltered life,' I told her.

'She sure has,' the President said. 'You know something? She was a nun.'

'She was a *what?*' No need for me to sound quite so surprised, but really!

Kiki threw back her head and laughed some more. 'He's crazy. Of course I wasn't a nun. I went to a convent school at Baton Rouge, and Gus thinks it's the same thing.'

Gus said doggedly, 'The way you told it, nuns came into it somewhere.'

'I was *taught* by nuns.'

'OK, so you were taught by nuns.' Gus glanced at Laurie and brightened. 'Say, did you know there was a character in Australia who once played fourteen rounds in a single day?'

Laurie said, 'His name was Stan Puckridge.' A good literary agent but a lousy diplomat.

The President studied her with a kind of wary respect. 'It was? I didn't know that.'

Laurie's cleaning lady was called Puckridge. Laurie's

cleaning lady's husband was called Stan. It could have been a coincidence but I doubted it. I wondered if this golf-mad African spent the whole of his spare time mugging up record books or if he got his facts out of Christmas crackers.

I said, 'Let's have the radio on. There's a weather forecast due just before the news.'

We listened to the forecast and we listened to the news. We rolled on in our lordly fashion towards Norfolk, as ill-assorted a golf foursome as you could wish for. In the police training manuals there is precious little on how to make light conversation with Heads of State of any kind, let alone their girlfriends. Chat was something one played strictly by ear and I could guess Laurie too was feeling her way. A lunatic couple we were escorting, not unlikeable, but unreal. Kiki and Gus and the Rolls and the Smith and Wesson weighing down my left shoulder, all unreal. Given another half an hour and I'd be back at my desk at Tiverton House and Laurie would be sorting out some hopeful writer's manuscript. Another half-hour and the yellow Rolls Corniche would turn itself back into a pumpkin.

Another half-hour and we were just east of Royston, Gus talking as usual.

'Carnoustie. We could go there next. Then St Andrew's, then Turnberry. You got that?'

How long, Oh Lord, how long? I was an indefinite attachment and there was nobody to appeal to. 'Yes,' I said. 'Got it.'

'Well, make a note, for Chrissake!'

Mine not to reason why. I felt in my pocket for something to write with and said a rudeness. Laurie looked over her shoulder. 'What have you lost?'

'My pen.'

'I got a pen,' Kiki said. She started to dig in her handbag.

I didn't want Kiki's pen, I wanted the cheap and cheerful ballpoint young Sam had bought me for my birthday. The fruit machine of memory clicked over and came up three in a row.

I said, 'I left it in the car.' I could see it, in the locker of the Khamsin.

'So it'll be there when you get back.' Kiki was holding out a gold thing to me.

'My car's in a garage having something done to it,' I told her. 'One of the mechanics will probably borrow it and forget to put it back.' It was true but it still sounded ridiculous.

Gus said, 'OK, call them up and tell the man to look out for this pen. You got the garage number?'

'Yes,' I said, 'I've got the number. I'll call them when I get to a phone.'

Kiki waved a cellular handset at me. 'Call them *now*, lover.'

I took the thing, feeling a fool for not having noticed it was there. After all, one didn't have to be a policeman to have a car phone these days, even a couple of tourists knew that. I prodded out the number of Peregrine Motors. It rang for a hell of a long time before someone answered.

'Is that you, Paddy?' It didn't particularly sound like Paddy but then it didn't sound like Oscar either.

'May I ask your name, sir?'

Most certainly not either of them. 'The name's Straun. Inspector Straun.'

Pause. Well, I could have got the wrong number. Irrationally I felt a fool trying to make sense in a mobile phone-box. Then the plastic against my ear said, '*Inspector Straun?*'

'Yes,' I said, 'Inspector Straun. Who's that?'

'Constable Baines, sir.'

For a moment I wondered if I'd rung Tiverton Street through force of habit, though I knew I hadn't. But I said,

'Is that Peregrine Motors? I wanted to speak to Oscar Louth.'

'You're on the right number, sir,' the voice of Constable Baines assured me. 'But I'm sorry about Mr Louth. He's dead. They're trying to—get him out now, sir.'

My phone-box slowed, went round a corner and accelerated away again. It was hard to get used to the idea that Oscar was dead, but the PC wasn't likely to be there for nothing. I said, 'What the hell happened to him?'

'We don't know, sir. Like I said, they're trying to get him out now.'

'Out from what, for God's sake?'

'The stove, sir.' There was a pause. Then: 'You should see it, sir. It's bloody horrible. But that's where he is. Inside the stove.'

CHAPTER 5

Even with death, the unfamiliar is the worst. For the victim it presumably doesn't matter all that much whether you're laid out in a chapel of rest or extruded through a mincer, but for the public at large the quality of the corpse is all-important. For myself, I didn't want Oscar dead at all, still less did I fancy the idea of him being compressed within the confines of a stove like some bizarre variety of canned chicken. Sickness is all. I gave up the unhappy Baines and as soon as we reached Thornton Basset and the decent privacy of the club's public phone I got on to Gareth Evans instead.

'A considerable trouble to those concerned, boyo.' His voice wasn't even sympathetic, probably because it was against his chapel principles to sound upset because what sounded like a rather tiresome killing had taken place on somebody else's patch.

I said, 'I was there where it happened, only this morning.' What was I saying? That I wanted to get myself involved?

'If Notting Hill wants a statement from you I'll let them know where you are.'

I stared at the phone numbers members had pencilled on the wall and wondered whose they were, while another part of my mind listened to my superior officer and still more admitted reluctantly that he was quite right. Cabel Gardens was nothing to do with Tiverton Street, and if anyone wanted to talk to me there was nothing to stop them. On the outside looking in, for once, no bad experience for a cop.

In my handset Gareth Evans's voice was saying, 'And how are our African friends enjoying themselves?'

I said, 'Better ask the Foreign Office. We're pretty hot on security.'

'Security, is it?' Evans Superintendent sounded un-amused. 'Diplomatic Corps, are we now?'

'If I am,' I said, 'it's not because I volunteered.'

'A holiday, then?' the maddening voice in my ear came back accusingly. 'Enjoying yourself, you are.'

'Well,' I said, 'you know Africans. Always ready for a party.'

I put the phone down before that started him off on the drink and driving bit. One thing to be said for Chapel, it gave one a lively sense of sin. Surprising there weren't more Welsh policemen, come to think of it. A natural affinity, like the Irish and the army.

I went in search of the secretary's office, feeling chastened and ill at ease. Physician, heal thyself. The sudden uncomfortable knowledge of what it was like to be an ordinary member of the public pleading with the police to do something. Well, I *was* the police and I wanted to know that something was being done to find Oscar's killer and all I'd got was a flea in my ear. The fact that this was what happened all too often to the general public was no comfort at all. What the hell, I thought, *you can't beat City Hall*. Oscar's dead and there's nothing you can do about it. You're here to play golf, so get on with it.

The Rogues' clubhouse was unexpectedly cosy, a sprawling, single-storeyed place faced in white-painted clapboard, the interior strong on chintz-covered sofas and good rugs on polished wood floors. What I could glimpse of the Members' Bar was all Spy cartoons and beer-engine handles, buttoned leather, copper and brass. I wondered if all this reflected the kind of homes the late Ernie Clarkson's outcasts had favoured, in which case it was all rather a let-down. Or was it that they all lived in the brash opulence of onyx jacuzzis and fibreglass oak beams? That way, their club was a kind of escape to a gentler world remembered from childhood, crumpets for tea and a teddy-bear by the fire.

Secretary, the neat lettering on the panelled door announced. *Colonel G. D. H. L. Blunt.*

'Come!'

I hadn't knocked. How had he known I was there? Anyway, I came. Colonel G. D. H. L. Blunt was sitting at a well-filled desk by the window, photographs of past club dignitaries on the walls, a side table with roses in a silver bowl. He stood up and offered me his hand.

'You're Angus Straun.'

I could have said, 'And you're Butcher Blunt,' but at a place like The Rogues it was hard to know if one was supposed to recognize people or not, so I shook the hand and said yes, I was. Geoffrey Blunt's fame, if you could call it that, went back a few years but he was still pretty recognizable as the mercenary commander who'd shot his way in and out of most of the world's nastier places, either setting up dubious governments or blasting them down, depending where the money came from. He'd got a face like a soldier on a war memorial plus a long scar that ran from high on his cheek to the corner of his mouth. I guessed he'd be about a seventy, but he still looked as though he'd be a handful to tangle with in the dark.

There was what looked like a blow-up of a news photograph on the wall just behind his head. Blunt in a bush jacket and beret, automatic rifle slung over his shoulder, among a group of self-consciously tough-looking characters, presumably fellow mercenaries. One very dark-haired soldier of fortune talking to his commander back to camera struck some very faint chord of memory, but no more. Apart from the fact that the background looked hot and dusty, there was no way of identifying it. Some trouble-spot. Angola, maybe, or South America.

I said, 'It's good of you to have us. Mr Aligar has been very much looking forward to playing here.'

'You are here as a member's guests, so naturally you are welcome.' I got the feeling that Blunt didn't exactly enthuse over the arrangement but then, we all have our troubles.

I said, 'Do we have a starting time?'

'You can play when you like. There are very few members about.' Blunt stared out of the window to confirm the fact or possibly give me a chance to admire the well-known chin-jutting profile. The last soldier of fortune or a dangerous psychopath, you took your pick. These days probably the latter, but that was just fashion. Mercenaries just sold their skills like anybody else. Interesting to have found him, all the same.

'I assume the professional takes the green fees?' I didn't presume anything of the kind but the least I could do was offer.

'There are no green fees.' Blunt brushed an invisible something off the sleeve of his hacking jacket. 'At The Rogues you don't buy a temporary membership, you are here as a guest. On the course, in the bar and in the dining-room. Just sign for anything you require.'

'That's very hospitable of you.'

'It's the tradition here.' Blunt bared his teeth slightly in what he presumably reckoned was a smile.

And while on the subject of traditions, I said tentatively, 'We have two ladies in our party.'

'My dear Straun, we have lady Rogues, I do assure you. No separate entrance here.'

'A weight off my mind.'

'You the Straun that was best amateur in—?'

'Yes.'

He nodded. 'Thought you might be. Have a good game.'

I went out making appreciative noises. The others were

prowling about the car park, studying whatever bits of the course were visible.

Gus said appreciatively, 'This is quite a place.'

I was inclined to agree with him. Up till now I'd been prepared to class The Rogues as a kind of joke, because in the nature of things when eccentrics get together they usually combine to produce something rather peculiar. But from what I could see of it, The Rogues Golf Club was everything rumour had claimed it to be. Norfolk is traditionally the flattest county in England and whoever had planned the course at Thornton Basset had been forced to work without benefit of a naturally undulating landscape. Most of the great Norfolk courses are links, marvellous stretches of sea grass between sand dunes with the wind howling in off the grey North Sea. This was a place sixty miles inland, a gentle stretch of parkland that looked so much like nature that it was hard to believe that the willows beside the lake must have been planted for Clarkson when he built the course, that the grove of tall ash that ran parallel to one of the fairways must have also been planted for Clarkson and that the hill at the far end of the lake was almost certainly the spoil from when they'd dug out old Ernie's pond. From where I stood, the fairways looked as manicured as those of Augusta, the rough an even six inches, the bunkers filled with white sand. Oh my America, my new found land! It was undoubtedly one hell of a golf course, no wonder the Rogues kept it to themselves. I just hoped that Gus wasn't going to take this as a norm, because St Andrew's was likely to be something of a let-down.

'All right,' I said, 'we'd better get changed. Meet at the first soon as you're ready.' I could have taken them to the hotel but, as we'd lunched on the way, that would have been a waste of time. I half-expected rebellion from the girls, but to my surprise they made agreeing noises, so we got our gear out of the Rolls and left her to the company of

a couple of Aston Martins, a black Silver Shadow and a
scattering of Jaguars and suchlike, which seemed to indicate
that if members lacked reputations they weren't doing so
badly on money. Laurie and Kiki headed off to their
locker-rooms, Gus and I to ours. I don't know what the girls'
was like, but ours was big, all mahogany and leather, brass
fittings in the showers and no smell of sweat and discarded
socks. What exactly did one have to do for membership? I
fished out my old black cashmere sweater with the darn in
one elbow and watched with interest as Gus unveiled a pair
of tartan trews and pulled them on without embarrassment.
I just hoped he doesn't plan to wear those at St Andrew's.
But at least they weren't Royal Stewart. So far as I could
make out they weren't anything, except a flight of fancy on
the part of the golf shop at Little Rock or wherever.

'Mixed foursomes?' I suggested. 'You and yours against
me and mine?' It came out pretty pat, how awful.

'Well, look—' Gus began.

We'd already exchanged handicaps, so I said, 'It should
work out fairly well. You're four and I'm six. Laurie plays
off twelve. What about Kiki?'

Pause. Some kind of machinery started up. A long way
away but presumably in the women's locker-room someone
flushed a loo.

Gus said, 'Kiki plays to scratch.'

No wonder there was a pause. 'Scratch?' An idiot-like
repetition. You heard the man. All the same, there weren't
all that number of ladies all that good. Not that many
men, for that matter. Where the hell had Kiki Bouchier got
herself a handicap like that since she left Louisiana?

'She's pretty good at ball games,' Gus said. 'I reckon it's
co-ordination, you know what I mean?'

'Yes,' I said, 'I know what you mean.' In fact, I didn't—
singing, in my book, having little to do with ball games.
But bully for Kiki, just the same. 'All right,' I said, 'so she's

our only scratch player. Laurie's a good twelve. A good twelve will make anyone sweat.' Well, perhaps not anybody, but me certainly. Laurie had taken up golf late but her father had been no mean player himself and she must have inherited the knack from him. She hit the ball a long way and off the ladies' tees it seemed even further. She was a fair twelve and as a somewhat dodgy six I found it hard to give her six strokes a round and leave myself with even a remote chance of winning.

Gus was fiddling with his shoelaces. 'I thought maybe you and I could play the girls. Might be kinda fun.'

I couldn't see why. 'Bit odd for a mixed foursomes, don't you think?'

'You don't get the point. She's one hell of a lot better than me.'

'If you play off four I shouldn't have thought—' I broke off as some kind of penny dropped. 'You did say your handicap was four, didn't you?'

Gus seemed to be having trouble getting his shoes on. 'Sure. It's just that—'

'Where?' It could hardly be his home course if it wasn't ready yet. Maybe in America?

'Well, there was this little place in New Jersey where some of the Embassy crowd played. I went along with them a few times and got pretty well hooked. Trouble was, I didn't get to go there very often.' Gus paused unhappily.

'So what happened?' I could guess what happened, but he might as well tell me.

'When I left the boys gave me a kind of farewell party, you know what I mean? And someone got this handicap certificate made out . . .' He sighed. 'OK, so it was a joke—'

'Look,' I said, 'you're not the first man to have improved his handicap a bit. No harm done. After all, you're the one that's going to be penalized. Real golf cheats try and pass themselves off as being *worse* than they really are.'

'You know, I didn't realize how hooked I was on the damn game till I was back home.' The President was looking up at me like a small boy trying to talk his way out of trouble. 'And how was I to know that Kiki played to scratch? Matter of fact, I've never actually played with her, so I thought that if you and I—'

'For God's sake,' I said, 'it's only a game!'

'Not to me it isn't,' Gus told me doggedly.

It was not unlike something from *The Bedside Book of Golfing Stories*: 'The Golf Addict in Full Cry'. Me, I'd grown up with the game so I'd never experienced the mind-blowing euphoria of the newly converted, the passion that makes the height of sexual lust no more than a mild distraction. But I'd seen it. I'd seen it.

'Even if you and I go out together,' I told him, 'Kiki is still going to see you play.'

'I know that,' Gus said, 'but I shan't be her partner, letting her down.' I wasn't sure how he'd got to be President, but I didn't imagine anyone had handed him the job on a plate. One thing for sure; good old Gus wasn't going to be in the same league when it came to golf or women.

I gave up. 'Have it your own way.' What was I, after all, but his humble bodyguard? Mine not to reason why, make sure the bugger doesn't die. I said, 'But while we're on the subject, do you happen to have a *real* handicap?'

Gus shook his head glumly. 'No.'

'Well, what do you go round in?' I nearly said, '*really* go round in', but that would have been cruel.

'The mid nineties, I guess.'

Say a pretty generous handicap of twenty. Well, he could have been worse. 'Look,' I said, 'we'll do it your way. You and I against the girls. All play level—no handicaps. So if you have an off day you have an off day.'

Gus looked grateful. 'I owe you.'

'I haven't solved a thing,' I told him. 'What are you going to tell her tomorrow?'

He didn't answer that.

'For God's sake,' I said, 'what does your handicap matter? I don't suppose Kiki minds if your golf is good, bad or indifferent.'

'You really think so?' Gus looked up at me quickly, eyes large and dark like a trusting hound. It was love all right. Not only was he golf mad, the poor bastard was besotted with his playmate, and no man can cope with more than one major emotional involvement at the same time, not even a Head of State.

'Well,' I said, 'I really hope so.' I wasn't any good at shoring up other people's depressed egos. Damn and blast Todhunter for getting me into this. 'Come on,' I said, 'we'll be keeping the girls waiting.'

And we were, unexpectedly. They were standing by the first tee with their clubs on hired electric trolleys, deep in discussing something or other like old buddies. A good-looking pair. I made suitably apologetic noises and outlined the partnering Gus and I had cooked up.

Laurie frowned. 'Isn't that a funny way to run a mixed foursomes?'

Well yes, a very funny way. Mixed foursomes were understood to be a mixed pair playing against another mixed pair, but as far as I knew there was nothing in the rules that said one couldn't play sex against sex. 'Yes,' I said briefly, 'but quite legal.'

'Well, that's all right then.' She was nothing if not quick on the uptake. God knows what she was thinking but whatever it was she didn't say.

'You want a trolley?' I asked Gus.

He shook his head.

'Well, I do.' With one dodgy shoulder I don't enjoy load-
ing myself down with a bag of clubs. Not good for the
image maybe but at least I'm still out there swinging after
thirty-six holes. I collected my wheels from an adequate
but by no means magnificent shop presided over by a bull-
shouldered Irishman who said his name was Timothy
Reagan. 'An' if your honour would be preferring a caddy I
can be after fetching one.'

No, I said, I didn't want a caddy. Given the chance, I'd have
liked to have known more about Mr Reagan, but stage
Irishmen always get me that way. But then at The Rogues one
would never know. Possibly he really was paid-up IRA. Cad-
dies I'd already suggested but the idea had been turned down.

When I got back Gus was making notes in a small book,
pleasure not standing in the way of business. He said, 'Now
we finally made it here, you'd better tell me what this place
has got that everywhere else hasn't.'

I looked down at the first fairway. Beyond the course the
austere Norfolk countryside shone beneath the wild light of
a winter sun. From somewhere on the right an erratic popping identified the local clay pigeon shoot. What the hell
was I supposed to say? That it had a perfect setting? That
it was exclusive? That there were a lot of trees, a lot of
flowering shrubs, a lot of water, none of which were there
by nature and must have been arranged in exchange for
some vast sum. A kind of miniature Augusta but more
usable. No question, the condition of the course was a mar-
vel. I pointed to a couple of groups of tiny figures, way off
in the distance. 'Well,' I said, 'for a start it hasn't got
people. In a golf-hungry country it's not often you can just
start a round in your own time. I could show you courses
that look as good as this in their own way but none that'll be
in as good condition. They're almost all of them overplayed.
Which is going to be your problem when you get back
home. Too many people wanting to play.'

'No problem,' Gus said. 'Build more courses.'

I could have pointed out that his country was rather more remote than, say, the Algarve, but why spoil a nice day? I said, 'We'll worry about that later. Best we get on with the game.'

Foursomes, mixed or otherwise, is quickish golf and good fun, inasmuch as you don't have to sort out your own mistakes. The game is between two sets of partners, one ball to each pair. Partners take it in turn to hit the thing, so it's always the other chap's fault if you get a rotten lie. If you're in luck, and the long hitter gets the drives and the wonder-worker with the short irons gets the tricky approach shots, it's possible to achieve impressive scores. But who gets to hit what is largely a matter of luck.

Kiki first. She selected a club from a vast and very professional bag and stood still, studying the hole for a moment, and very good she looked. At least her handicap hadn't been arrived at in the same way as Gus's. Even with 375 yards straight ahead of her to an elevated bunker-protected green, she wasn't likely to be worried. A top tour lady she may not have been, but there's still a great gulf fixed between scratch folk and the rest. She took her dinky blue-headed driver, waggled it gently behind the ball a couple of times and socked it. Wow!

'Great shot!' I said. I wasn't looking at the ball as much as her swing. Well, as much as her. She looked like something out of a how-to-do-it book, hands high, that incredible body stretched into an arc, her follow-through practically smacking her bottom. When I got around to looking at the ball it was still climbing, climbing into the rain-washed East Anglian sky. When it finally got around to dropping it fell slap in the middle of the fairway, two hundred yards on. Kiki Bouchier may not have made a million on the ladies' golf circuit but she could hit a ball all right.

'You go,' said Gus.

Well, that made sense, because if Gus was to perform at all, the shorter the better. I risked my driver and got away with it, maybe twenty yards beyond Kiki and straight enough. I stared after the ball and felt a certain sense of achievement. At least I'd got my man to his damn club. The Foreign Office could congratulate itself on the fact that we were at this moment actually starting a game. We picked up our bits and pieces and headed off into the wild blue yonder.

Kiki's ball was sitting in a rare divot hole in the middle of the fairway with 175 yards to go. Laurie's turn, and I could guess how she felt. The responsibility of taking over a perfect lie, the 12-handicapper following someone off scratch. As it happened, it may have worried me but it certainly didn't seem to matter to her as she bent down and moved her ball to the grass at the side of the scrape.

'Hi!' Gus protested. 'You can't do that! First rule of golf is you play the ball as it lies.'

'Winter Rules,' Laurie told him composedly. 'There was a notice by the first tee. We get preferred lies.'

Gus blinked. 'I never heard of Winter Rules.' Well, he wouldn't, would he? Africa probably had local rules about elephants but winter was hardly a hazard in those parts.

'The game's different under winter rules,' I told him.

Gus said, 'I can see that. How come?'

'It's to protect the fairways, so that people don't hack them to bits in bad weather, trying to get out of impossible lies.' I tried to remember where it all came in the little green book. 'You'll find it all under *Local Rules*. If you don't like your lie you can shift it six inches, just so long as it's not nearer the hole. You can get away with murder.'

Gus nodded. 'Great! I got it.' He smiled at Laurie. 'Go hit the thing, ma'am. Sorry to hold you up.'

'You're welcome.' Laurie pushed a lock of hair out of her eyes, took a 3 wood and swung with an elegance that

equalled her partner's. The ball dropped in front of the two
left-hand bunkers, bounced neatly between them and rolled
to the heart of the green. She didn't look surprised. I caught
her eye. Did she smile ever so slightly? Laurie, my love, I
don't suppose you could do that again, but what the hell,
you're not supposed to do it twice.

'Right,' I said. 'Follow that, Gus.'

We walked on to my ball which must have been 150
yards from the pin, and the President tentatively selected a
5 iron. Well, if that wouldn't do, nothing would.

'Nice and slow,' I said.

He took hold of the club and squared up to the ball.
Nobody could have said that chunk of a body looked
relaxed, but at least someone had taught him about the
overlapping grip. He took the clubhead back painfully
slowly, but his wrists cocked and came down reasonably
smoothly. A small divot shot up but so, thank God, did the
ball. I followed its flight with as much relief as he must
have done. It carried about a hundred and twenty yards,
got an unlucky bounce and landed in a bunker.

'Hard luck,' Laurie said. I hadn't had a chance to have
a word with her but some form of female radar had told
her how the land lay. I could sense Gus's moment of blissful
relief. He'd hit the ball well enough. Anyone can land in a
bunker.

Laurie had hit her ball within a couple of feet of the hole
so I told Kiki to pick it up. After all, this was match play
and it was a fair gimme. I hardly imagined I could get in
from the bunker, and I couldn't.

One up to the girls.

The second at The Rogues is a dogleg, 486 yards off the
back tees and a justified Par 5. The direction of the fairway
is to the right, the angle filled with a miniature pine forest
into which the slicer vanishes, never to return. On the left,
roughish rough but better than trees. Laurie drove, tried

too hard and pushed it either into or at least on the very
edge of the pines. Gus, faced with a drive, resisted the
temptation he must have felt to try his luck with a wood
and instead chose a 3 iron. My respect for him went up a
couple of points. Given the chance, I suspected that the
man might even end up playing the game.

His Excellency swung and muttered something under
his breath. Understandably, as he'd hit the ball hard
enough but hooked it. I made sympathetic noises and we
trudged off towards the rough to an accompaniment of
pops from the clay shoot. Laurie and Kiki made for the
wood.

Gus said, 'I was a fool to get involved in this game.' He
seemed to think it was an original thought.

'Look,' I told him, 'you're doing fine. Just take it
easy.'

'I landed myself in the rough, God dammit.'

'Well, the girls are in the trees, so we've both got problems.' I glanced over my shoulder. Laurie was walking
along the edge of the wood, Kiki was inside it. I took an
iron out of my bag and started prodding the rough. Some
kind of bird took off from under my feet with a mighty
flapping of wings.

'Got to be here somewhere,' Gus said, the cry of the
dedicated golfing man. He swung his club at the under-
growth and must have hit something because there was a
metallic clang. He grunted with satisfaction. 'Here.'

But he was wrong. Still no ball. And then suddenly I saw
it. Not in the rough but in deep sand on the edge of the
fairway. A bunker.

I said, 'And where the devil did that come from?' A not
unfair question as it had seemed to have appeared out of
the blue. Happily, The Rogues supplied rather splendid
score cards backed with miniature plans of each hole, and
sure enough the bunker was real all right. It was called

Tricky Dickie, and after a second look I saw why. The infernal thing was back to front, its cavernous sandy depths facing the hole instead of the tee, so that for anyone who hadn't done his homework it constituted a virtually invisible hazard.

I looked across the fairway and saw that Laurie was signalling to her partner that she had found their ball. Kiki emerged from the wood with evident relief, took what looked like a long iron and drove it high over the trees towards the unseen leg. It was a risky shot but if it came off was going to save them at least a stroke. It came off.

'She's good,' I said.

Gus nodded mournfully. 'Bright girl. Like that with everything.'

'Nobody's like that with everything,' I told him. I looked at my ball philosophically.

Gus looked guilty. 'Sorry about that.'

'No sweat.' I went back to my trolley and fished out my sand iron.

The grip felt odd, which wasn't right because I'd had a new one fitted only a week or so ago. What the hell? I held the thing up. A burn, a channel seared across the rubber a couple of inches above the chrome of the shaft.

'What's the matter?' Gus was looking at me curiously.

I said, 'There's something wrong with my grip.' I bent down and looked at my bag. On one side a small, neat hole. On the other side a small, neat hole. I was good on small, neat holes. A bullet goes in one side, sears the grip of the nearest club, exits on the other side. I straightened up slowly. Shit. This was what I was here for, to look after a distinguished African politician. We had played one hole and already someone had taken a pot shot at him. True, he'd missed and hit my golf bag instead, but there were another seventeen holes to go.

'Sit down,' I said.

'Sit?' Gus looked at me blankly.

I said, 'Sit down, for Chrissake! Someone's shooting at you!'

CHAPTER 6

'OK.' Gus sat down unhurriedly, fortunately not one given
to hysteria. He looked around with no more than a polite
interest. 'They shot from those trees over there?'

'Probably.'

'Someone on that skeet shoot firing a bit wild?'

It would have been nice to believe it. I pointed to the
hole in my bag. 'Does that look like a twelve-bore?'

The girls were between us and the trees. I didn't like the
idea of them crossing the open fairway but on the other
hand they were probably in even more danger where they
were. I waved them over. They came, looking as though
they were being called to help find a lost ball.

'What's he sitting down for?' Kiki wasn't asking Gus, she
was asking me.

'Someone took a shot at him.' I mentally cursed the Todhunters and the Gareth Evanses of this world who would
cook up this kind of situation. Security cover is a kind of
diplomatic courtesy that persuades this or that president
that he is important enough for someone to want to kill
him. But if Gus Aligar was really a candidate for the chop,
even a genuine paid-up member of Special Branch wasn't
going to be enough to guard him. How does one guard a
man with a hand gun while some nut stalks him with tele-
scopic sights over a high velocity rifle?

'We'd better get back to the clubhouse,' Laurie said.

Well, yes. Only it suddenly seemed a long way to walk
along that unprotected fairway. I had an uncomfortable
picture of Gus standing out in firm black silhouette while
somebody lined him up. I wondered what a real Special
Branch type would do in the same situation. Easy to answer

that. No Special Branch man would have let his charge
loose on a golf course in the first place. I fished in the pocket
of my bag and brought out my own pair of Leitz roof prism
miniature binoculars and took a good look at the trees from
which the shot must have come. I asked the girls if they'd
heard anything.

'Only the guns at the skeet shoot,' Kiki said. 'There's a
road pretty near, too.'

I'd forgotten the road. No particular reason why someone
shouldn't have shot from there—except the fact that the
trees would have been in the way. I swung the glasses along
the copse, lingering over the shadows and then on towards
the clubhouse. So far I hadn't seen another living thing,
and even a close-up of the car park didn't reveal anyone
stirring. There was something odd about the car park just
the same and I had to go on staring for several seconds
before the penny dropped.

Gus's yellow Rolls wasn't there any more.

To have got my charge shot at and to have let someone
pinch his car in my very first day as a watchdog had to be
something of a record. I broke the news as gently as I could.

'Missed me, got the car,' Gus observed philosophically.
'At least he makes a profit on the day.'

He'd been pretty good about the whole thing but I could
cheerfully have hit him, this being no time for the flip one-
liner. I said shortly, 'You and Kiki get back to the
clubhouse. Laurie and I will keep between you and the
wood.'

Gus frowned. 'Hey, that's not on. Your girl—'

'Laurie doesn't mind.' Of course Laurie didn't mind.
Healthy girls probably liked acting as a screen against lunatic gunmen and I didn't propose asking her in case she
didn't. So for good or ill we headed back to the clubhouse,
two couples with about a dozen yards between us. It seemed
a long way. I could see Gus muttering to his girl as he

walked. Perhaps after all I was over-reacting. After all, if
the President didn't mind being shot at, why was I getting
in a state?

Beside me, Laurie said, 'Are you absolutely sure that
shot wasn't an accident?'

'No,' I said, 'I'm not. But I'm damned if I'm taking any
chances.'

Laurie frowned, a sign of concentration rather than
actual disapproval. 'If there is someone stalking us we must
be stuck up like those ducks at shooting galleries.'

I said, 'I don't think there is anyone stalking us. I think
whoever it was has cleared off in Gus's Rolls.' I waited for
her to ask why he hadn't got a car of his own, which was
what I was asking myself, but she didn't. Perhaps she felt
it was too much like potting a sitting target. Anyway, she
didn't speak again until we reached the car park without
further excitement.

The yellow Rolls had gone all right. The Jaguar that had
been parked alongside it was still there, as was the handful
of cars that had been in the car park when we arrived. No
owners, no chauffeurs. A silver BMW had a white Cairn
terrier stretched out on the shelf behind the back seats but
even he was asleep.

Gus said, 'Back home, nobody would even think of this.
Not even *think* of it.' He was far more concerned about
losing his hired Rolls than he had been about someone
taking a shot at him.

'Console yourself at the bar,' I said. 'I'll have a word
with the secretary.'

Back to Butcher Blunt, who didn't seem particularly
pleased to see me.

'Someone's what?'

I said, 'Someone's stolen President Aligar's car.'

The rough-hewn face twitched and those astonishing pale

blue eyes bored into mine. 'Don't talk bloody nonsense. He's forgotten where he put it, that's all.'

In police basic training they teach one how to get on with the public. I wasn't all that good at it, but I tried. 'Look, I was there when he parked it,' I said. 'The car is no longer there.'

Blunt didn't respond. 'So what the hell do you want me to do? Order the members to turn out their pockets?'

'Yes, if I tell you to.' Objectionable sod. I said, 'You know I'm a policeman, so you can assume I'm not making this up. I'm not suggesting a member of this club has stolen the car, but I'd like to know if you've had any trouble of this kind before.'

Blunt's stubby fingers drummed the desk in front of him. 'No.'

'Any break-ins? Vandalism? That kind of thing?'

'If there had been, the police would have been informed.'

Well, maybe. You'd have to be bright to put it over on the Rogues, who probably had a trick or two of their own and it was all too easy to imagine Butcher Blunt dealing personally with anyone caught breaking and entering their clubhouse. The bastinado was the least you could expect if caught with your trousers down at Thornton Basset.

'Yes,' I said, 'I expect they would.' I did my best to sound unconvinced.

Blunt stood up and I thought what a stocky little man he was. Odd how often small men were aggressive. Well, perhaps not all that odd but surprising that they should be so consistent about it. I waited for the action but it seemed there wasn't going to be any. 'Sorry. Wasn't suggesting you were imagining things. It's just that it's a bit unusual. I mean—miles from anywhere like this. You'd expect members' cars to be safe enough.' Blunt rearranged the paperweights on his desk. He was a great fiddler. 'Look, why don't you get on with your round. Leave this to me.

Just give me the details of the car and I'll have a word with the police.'

Pause. Well, why not? We were guests of the club, after all. A good secretary wouldn't want us to spoil our day, and car thefts were not the proper business of Special Branch. I said, 'That's very civil of you.'

'Glad to help,' Blunt said. 'If you take my advice, you'll go out and finish your round. The local police are remarkably efficient. Chances are they'll have your car back by the time you get to the nineteenth.'

I went in search of the bar and my companions.

'Well?' An uncompromising lot, always wanting answers.

'The secretary says the car will be back by the time we finish our round.'

Laurie blinked. 'He's that sure?'

'Major Blunt's reported it. He has confidence.'

So, as a matter of fact, had I. I wasn't any great shakes on the car theft business but I did know that Highway Patrols held details of all cars stolen in their area for at least twenty-four hours, and there weren't likely to be all that many Rolls Corniches running around the roads of Norfolk at any one time.

'So that's great,' Gus said. 'Now, suppose we finish our round?' Pause for raised eyebrows. What was I drinking? I was drinking Scotch and glad of it.

'Cheers,' I said. 'But wasn't the first leg exciting enough for you?'

Gus thought that over. 'Hell,' he announced finally, 'lightning never strikes the same place twice. Correct?'

'I don't know,' I said. 'You'd better look in your bumper book of records.' In the same circumstances a British politician would have been amenable to reason, which was a polite way of saying he'd be taking the first train home. But I didn't know about Africans. I certainly didn't know about Gus, amiably unlike anything I'd been led to expect. No

wonder he'd been able to dispense with a proper bodyguard, Special Branch had seen him coming. At least it was
no longer a surprise they'd unloaded him on to me.

Kiki drew a cashmere cardigan about her elegant shoulders. 'Me, I'm all for finishing, now we've come all this
way. Who knows? Could just have been someone at the
skeet shoot fooling around.'

Which was exactly what Laurie had said. Well, people
did the maddest things with firearms and it was possible
that some maniac could have let fly at a rabbit with a
high velocity rifle. Well, just possible. It was a damn silly
situation anyway, because officially Gus could dispense
with my services any time he liked. I couldn't force myself
on him, equally I didn't relish the prospect of reporting in
due course that I'd stood by and allowed my charge to get
himself assassinated. But I was damned if I was going back
to Todhunter to seek his fatherly advice.

'Drink up!' Gus was saying. He may not have known
much about golf clubs but he was picking up the language
at commendable speed.

I was making mildly protesting noises when Butcher
Blunt came through the door.

'Glad I caught you before you went out again.' He ran
his eyes briskly over the girls. 'I haven't met your friends.'
His old African mates wouldn't have known him.

I did the necessary and Blunt raised a finger to the bar
steward and ordered a round. After my initial reception it
was not unlike being stuck in a pub with the spirit of Christmas Present. When we were clutching fresh glasses he said,
'I've just had a call from your colleagues, Straun. They've
got the Rolls back. Just like I said, no trouble.'

No wonder he was so cheery. 'That's a weight off our
minds,' I said.

'Told you it wouldn't take long.' It was his police force
now, not mine.

I said, 'Do you happen to know where they picked him up?'

Blunt nodded. 'Just this side of Mereham, I think. Some young fool joy-riding. They're bringing it back right away.'

'The car's all right?' I had to ask the question but dreaded the answer because cars retrieved from joy-riders rarely are. At the very least the radio is ripped out and more often than not the car itself has ended up in a ditch. It was no wonder Rolls insurance cover was astronomic. You get very few body scratches on their sort of paintwork for a thousand pounds.

Blunt said cheerfully, 'Not a scratch on it. They got the young tearaway, too. Walking along the road, just after he'd dumped it.'

'He hadn't run it into a telegraph post or anything?'

'No.'

'Then why had he left it?' Well, why had he? Joy-riders only left the cars they'd nicked when they'd crashed them or run out of petrol.

Blunt frowned. 'Christ, I don't know. You'll have to ask the chaps who picked him up. They're bringing the car back here. Perhaps the ladies would like some tea.'

'How kind,' Kiki said. Blunt eyed her meditatively. Perhaps he was thinking that in the good old days she'd have been part of the rape and pillage, but eventually he called a steward and in spite of Gus's obvious impatience we sat around in the sun eating cucumber sandwiches while the Butcher made polite conversation about the roses until an orange-striped white Rover arrived, closely followed by the missing Rolls. The four of us went out to meet it. Blunt stayed behind.

'You don't want to leave these things lying about, you know,' the young constable told me as he climbed out. 'It's tempting tearaways, that's what it is.' His companion behind the wheel of the Rolls nodded agreement.

I said, 'I'm afraid it's not mine. But it was locked.'
I showed him my warrant card. 'And the radio's still
there?'

'Yes, sir.' The PC was giving me a crafty going-over, not
surprising as coppers playing at The Rogues must have
been about as common as hen's teeth. 'Funny thing, now
you mention it.'

I got into the Rolls and looked round. So far as I could
see, it was much as we'd left it, radio still there, likewise
the phone. I prodded the latter inexpertly into life and
caught the constable's inquiring eye. 'Got the operator all
right,' I said. 'It still works.'

'Lucky, sir. Very.' He jerked his head towards the Rover,
where I caught a glimpse of a rather good-looking youth in
the back. 'That's our boy, over there. Name of Miller, works
locally as stable-boy. Want to have a word?'

A handsome offer, but reluctantly I shook my head. It
was damn-all to do with me, after all. Besides, restraint is
a statesman-like virtue and I was playing at being Special
Branch today. 'No,' I said, 'I'll leave that to your chaps.
But how did you come to pick him up?'

'Dunno. Chance, really.' The PC wasn't one to overstate
his case. 'PC Leathers and me spotted the Roller at the
same time. On this bank and empty. Locked and all. Jimmy
Leathers reckoned the owner must have got caught short
and nipped into the wood while he'd got time, so we pushed
on. Then we spots this young hopeful legging it along the
open road, bloody miles from anywhere. Well, it stood to
reason he'd come from the car. We stopped and I told him
to turn his pockets out. He'd got the Roller's key.'

'You did all right.' Americanized, but what else to say?
Good show, Leathers, I knew you had it in you?

'Thank you, sir.'

Well, at least he'd used his head. Easy enough not to
have been curious about the parked car in the first place,

easy to have ignored the solitary walker. I said, 'What time was this?'

'I filed a report at fourteen thirty-five, sir.'

'And when had you heard the car was missing?'

The constable grinned. 'We hadn't, sir. As a matter of fact, the description of the Rolls as a missing car came through while we were questioning the suspect.'

Better and better. Leathers would go places. 'What was his story?'

'Said he'd always wanted to know what a Rolls was like so he took it for a run.'

'Taking without permission?'

'That's right, sir,' Leathers agreed. 'Just a joy-ride.'

Well, of course it could have been. But in that case what had possessed whoever it was to abandon the thing five miles from the nearest town?

I left Leathers to it and walked back to where Laurie was waiting for me.

'So why ring the operator?' She'd been close enough to hear what I'd been saying, and Laurie Wilson was nobody's fool.

I said, 'I wasn't ringing the operator. If you must know, I was recalling the last dialled number, in case our joy-rider had been making a call home.'

'And had he?'

'I shouldn't think so.' It had been a hopeful moment but, like most hopeful moments, fleeting. I said, 'All I got was some Merseyside lady who only got as far as "Hello" before we got cut off. Or someone slammed the phone down.' I wasn't over worried. 'It doesn't matter,' I explained. 'The number's safe in the phone's memory. I'll get it traced easily enough.'

Laurie said, 'He was probably only phoning Mum.'

'Probably,' I said.

But, in fact, the idea of Mick the Miller phoning his

grey-haired old mother in the middle of a job was quite the most improbable idea I'd heard that day. Still, the Rolls was back and Gus was pleased. One couldn't have everything.

CHAPTER 7

And so to the bar for a celebratory drink, what else? Butcher Blunt was already there, together with half a dozen members, and he bought us a round, all smiles.

'Pleased it got cleared up so quickly. Bad for the club, a thing like that.'

A fortyish blonde lady who must have been sensational at twenty and was still by no means a troll put down her glass and said, 'Bad for young Mick, too. Silly little bugger.'

'You're right, Rosie.' Sympathetic mutters, murmured introductions. Lady Rosemary Luton. Lady Captain this year. For some reason I hadn't cottoned on to the fact that there might be lady Rogues, but why not in these egalitarian times? Rosie Luton was rather well dressed in a yellow cashmere sweater and a tan check skirt that was kind to a satisfying if slightly generous figure. She clutched a strong Scotch in a practised way but a fit lady with a name that rang some kind of bell.

'Miller's one of Rosie's stable-boys,' someone said obligingly. 'Rides for her too, sometimes.'

Ah! Rosemary Luton, wife of racehorse owner Sir Andrew Luton. Née Lady Rosemary Duttington, a legendary wild gal and something to do with a rather messy divorce case. Probably a very well-qualified Rogue when one came to think of it. We milled around a bit and I found myself up against her, not, I imagine, by accident.

'Look,' she said, 'you know about these things. What the hell do I do about Micky?'

'Micky?'

'Michael O'Shaugnessy Miller.' She didn't exactly stamp

her foot but the clipped, A.1. diction took on an edge. 'My idiot Irish serf.'

Of course. That Miller. 'I should leave him to stew a bit if I were you,' I told her. 'Won't do him any harm. Might do him a bit of good, come to that.'

Rosie Luton frowned. 'Don't be such a hard bastard. The poor lamb must be scared out of his wits.'

I said, 'I'm not a hard bastard, just a policeman. And if your lamb doesn't like what's happened to him, he should keep his sticky fingers off other people's cars.'

'I know. I know.' She had a quick swallow. 'Do you think they'll be giving him a bad time?'

'You mean, are the local officers beating him up?'

Her big blue eyes sought mine. 'Well, he *is* Irish. One hears—'

'One shouldn't believe all one hears, you know.'

She sighed. 'I suppose I've been rude.'

'Let's say you're upset.' Commendable restraint. Still, I could hardly lambast her in her own bar, more's the pity.

She grinned unexpectedly. 'Sorry. But he's quite the most beautiful thing you ever did see.'

Well, an honest troll at that. Probably a founder female Rogue. I said, 'Well, you'd better get him some legal advice. But a spot of joy-riding is no capital offence, you know. You can always pay his fine.'

'But then he'll have a criminal record and they won't let him have a visa for America.'

'Vital?'

'Important, anyway. I've a horse running in three races there come April. Over the sticks. Mick's supposed to be riding her.'

There was the odd approving noise from someone over-hearing Rosie's revelations. I gathered that the horse was well thought of, probably Miller, too. The Irish, known to have their little ways, are proverbially good with horseflesh.

Rosie Luton was fixing me with those blue eyes of hers and doing her best not to make them steely. She said, 'Please, Inspector. Go and see him.'

I don't know what it was I'd expected but not quite that. I said, 'What on earth for?'

She didn't seem a woman who was often at a loss, but the whole business had thrown her. She said, 'God, I don't know. Just see if there's anything he wants. If he's all right.'

'If he's still in one piece, you mean.'

'No,' she said, 'I didn't mean that. It's just, well—'

'Look, Lady Luton—'

'For God's sake, call me Rosie. We're all friends here.'

I said, 'All right, Rosie, friends we are. But I'm nothing to do with the police in this part of the world. Can't go digging into their business. It's just not done.'

She thought that one over. They thought it over. Over my shoulder Gus said, 'Unofficially, maybe. To oblige a lady?'

There were all kinds of things I could have said to that, including a suggestion that he should mind his own business. But, God help me, I had Todhunter and the Foreign Office breathing down my neck. Lord, what cowards we mortals be. The things we do for the sake of an easy life.

'You realize,' I said, 'that if I go to see this character, that's it. I can talk to him, see if there's anything he wants. But I can't get him out.'

Rosie Luton rewarded me with a dazzling smile. 'Understood.'

'Then what do you want me to say to him?'

'Just give him my love.' She seemed to think that one over for a moment, then shrugged her shoulders and looked back at me. 'Leave that embarrassing Rolls where it is. I'll take you in my car.'

*

She had some sort of Japanese convertible with the top unseasonably down. It was less draughty than I'd expected even though she drove me to Thornton Basset nick far too fast, though with some skill. She showed no sign of wishing to accompany me, so I went in alone to try my luck. A policeman off his own patch is an unloved thing, but they could only say no.

'The taking and driving away?' I'd introduced myself and the station sergeant seemed pleased to have some business. 'The name's Miller, Michael O'S.'

I said, 'Like Mick the Miller.'

'Sir?'

'He was a greyhound,' I told him. 'Before your time.' Before my time too, come to that.'

'I see, sir.' Clearly he didn't see but was too polite to say so. 'May I ask your interest in the prisoner?'

'Prisoner?'

The sergeant rearranged the day book in front of him. 'We're holding him till the CID sergeant gets over from Alton. I gather it was a CD car.'

I said, 'Actually it was a hired car driven by someone with diplomatic status.' I enlarged on this and the sergeant was visibly impressed. 'You want to see him, sir?'

'Quite unofficially.'

'You go ahead. If anyone says anything I'll tell them to refer to Special Branch.'

I nodded, as though I was sure that would do some good, and I was given a PC to escort me to the interview room and Mick the Miller.

'My name is Inspector Straun.' I sat down facing him at the plain varnished table and we had a look at each other. He was a lean young man in his early twenties, wearing the appropriate uniform of windcheater, jeans and trainers. He had dark hair, bony wrists and vivid blue eyes, a quite astonishingly good-looking lad whose face gave no hint of any form of depravity, which was just as well. I wasn't fooled and I doubted if Rosie Luton was either. But why look below the surface if you're getting value for money?

Miller didn't return the introduction. His eyes were turned towards me but it would be a wild exaggeration to say that he was looking at me. Those bright eyes were neither bold nor shifty, one felt they looked far beyond the confines of Thornton Basset nick to the green hills and the light clouds scudding above County Clare.

I said, 'What about a cup of coffee?'

'That's kind of you.'

'Smoke?'

He nodded and I looked round at the PC who had stationed himself at the far end of the room and was watching impassively.

'He can have one of mine, sir.' It wouldn't be one of his, but it was the constable's role to be the friendly chap. He even lit it for Miller before departing to fetch two plastic cups of coffee.

'Been in trouble before?' I asked.

There was a brief pause before the answer, presumably while he worked out that this was something I could check up on anyway.

'A couple of times there have been. Yes, there have.'

'Taking and driving away?'

'That's it.'

'But not for some time.'

No, he agreed. Not for some time.

'So,' I asked, 'why now?'

'It was a fine-looking car, sure enough.'

Well, yes, that thing sitting there just waiting to be nicked. It must have been a temptation. 'Look,' I said, 'have you ever driven a Wraith before?'

The boy sighed. 'It wasn't a Wraith I was taking. It was a Corniche.'

'Was it? I can't tell one from another,' I told him. 'I suppose this was the latest one?'

'Three years old.'

I asked him what they were like to drive. He claimed to have driven most types of Rolls at one time or another and he gave me a quite spirited account of his experiences. He was, it appeared, a keen supporter of the marque and in different circumstances would probably have been a prominent member of the Rolls-Royce Owners' Club. His theoretical knowledge seemed unlimited and he reeled off weights, speeds, power curves and whatever with unthinking authority. It was something of an achievement for one whose experience had been joy-riding in cars taken without their owners' permission.

I broke in on his dissertations reluctantly because they were quite informative and he seemed to be enjoying himself, nevertheless there was something I wanted to know. 'By the way, Mick—that car this afternoon. How did you get in?'

He grinned. 'Would it be difficult, now, with the key in the lock and the door open?'

It's lucky I have a reasonably controlled copper's face or I'd have looked as startled as I felt. I hadn't even thought to ask Gus if he'd locked the thing. Why hadn't I? Because like anyone else I could forget the obvious.

Mick said soothingly, as though reading my thoughts, 'Sure and it's happening all the time.'

Well, yes. And that was one of the reasons London alone had six figures of cars stolen every year. I swallowed some of the awful coffee in order to hide my feelings, and wondering why I was feeling guilty anyway. It wasn't my car and I hadn't been driving it. Was I my brother's keeper? No, I most certainly was not, so I looked cheerful. 'It must have been your lucky day.'

'It'll be my lucky day when they let me out of here.' Mick

drew gratefully on the PC's cigarette. He eyed me craftily. 'Now, do you think that will be soon?'

'It shouldn't be long,' I told him. 'After all, it isn't as if you did any damage.'

He looked quite shocked. 'And for what would I be wanting to harm a fine car like that?'

'I didn't want to hurt your feelings,' I assured him. 'But all the same, I'm surprised you didn't take the radio.'

Mick sighed. 'Now have you ever tried to get the radio out of a Rolls?'

'Frankly,' I confessed, 'no.'

'Well, a terrible job it is, to be sure. A man's having to take the car to pieces before he can start.'

One learns something every day but I tried not to show it. I said, 'You left the car a couple of miles from anywhere when you could have dumped it in a car park and been a lot nearer home.'

Sure and I'd been misunderstanding him, you could see the puzzlement in his honest blue eyes. 'Didn't I see the blue lamp of the patrol car sticking up over the hedgerows when it was a mile away? 'Get out while you can,' I said to myself, and started walking.'

'And much good it did you.'

'Much good indeed.' Mick looked round hopefully. 'Would there be a chance of another cigarette?'

I got up to go. 'You'll have to ask your friend,' I said. 'I don't smoke.'

'You'll have a long life.'

'I plan to,' I said. 'God bless all here.'

Rosie Luton dropped me off at the Bell, grateful in the assurance that her lover was not being gone over with lengths of hosepipe but still leaving me with the uncomfortable feeling that I had come off second best, but then, who does anything else when talking to the Irish? The others

were in the bar by the time I arrived, and I swallowed one
drink and then we went in to dinner. The restaurant was
all oak beams and pink lampshades, but for about a week's
wages one could eat pretty well.

'Nice,' Gus said. He meant it too, a most rewarding chap.
He was wearing a dark flannel suit with a white shirt and
some kind of club tie, showing a restraint that some of the
other diners might well have followed. Kiki was also suitably covered with something simple and expensive and my
heart warmed to them, making a note of the fact that
although I wished I might be somewhere else it still was
not their fault. Mr Todhunter's fault perhaps, but definitely
not theirs.

Kiki asked if I'd found out why 'that young man' had
stolen Gus's car.

'For fun,' I told her. 'He just wanted to drive the thing.'

She frowned. 'What will happen to him?'

Not the first to ask that question, nor the last. 'Very
little,' I told her. 'A lecture from the magistrate. Probation
maybe.'

Her extraordinary dark eyes opened a bit wider. 'Is that
all? For stealing a hundred thousand dollar car?'

'He didn't steal it,' I told her. 'He just took it away
without the owner's permission.'

'So what's the difference?'

I said, 'He simply has to swear that he didn't mean to
keep the car permanently. We couldn't prove theft unless
we caught him selling the thing.'

She blinked. 'But, man, that's crazy!'

I looked at Gus. 'So is leaving the keys in the lock. Miller
couldn't believe his luck.'

He had the grace to look sheepish. 'You know, I thought
about that just a while back, when I was checking the car
was OK.'

I felt a twinge of unease. 'Checking?'

Gus nodded. 'Sure. But like you said, no trouble. Even rang through on the phone to get a time check. Works fine.'

And that would have killed the phone's memory of Miller's call, I thought resignedly. My fault—I should have got someone working on a trace earlier. I must have looked savage at that moment because Gus said apologetically, 'Gee, I'm real sorry about the key. Forgot I was not at home.'

'Don't people steal cars where you come from?'

The President showed all those white teeth again. 'Yes, indeed they do. But not from me.'

Well, no, I suppose not. I said, 'No harm done, fortunately. But try to remember while you're here you don't get preferential treatment.'

Gus nodded. 'Back home soon, anyway.'

I said, 'I'm sorry.' In fact I wasn't, but he was a nice chap.

'Why not come out and have a look at my course for yourself?' He caught Laurie's eye. 'Both of you, naturally.'

The ever-present problem of how to reply to the unwanted invitation. All very well to advocate an honest answer because an honest answer has never turned away wrath. And in any case it wasn't as though I had anything against Gus or even his country, about which I knew absolutely nothing. I just didn't want to go.

I said, 'It's a kind thought but I don't think it would go down too well with the DC.'

Kiki meshed the fingers of her left hand with the right. They looked about ten inches long plus, say, two inches of scarlet nail. 'I guess Gus could fix that.'

She looked at Gus and he nodded amiably. 'Sure.'

I smiled, probably not convincingly. 'I'm afraid it's not as easy as all that.' But I had an uncomfortable feeling that it might be.

Kiki was giving me one of those come-on looks which

could better have been done elsewhere. I doubt if Gus spotted it but Laurie did and I looked elsewhere.

'Your Foreign Office has been real nice,' Gus was saying. 'They'll spare you for a few days more. No problem.' He looked amiably at Laurie.

'I'd love it,' Laurie said. 'Nothing I'd enjoy more, but there are things to do. I'm afraid it's just not on.'

'Do the things another time.' He could be persuasive, could Gus. Authoritative, too.

'I've a client coming from Ireland to see me.' She managed to make it sound as though it were not an excuse, no small feat in the circumstance. 'I'm sorry, Gus.'

An air of stickiness all round, which even the excellence of the food couldn't quite ungell, a relieved retreat to our respective rooms, fourposter et al. In it, we lay contemplating its silken roof, a moment in which to contemplate the nonsenses of the day, that pleasant ritual. Perhaps not so on this occasion.

After a while Laurie said, 'What possessed you to book us in here?'

It wasn't the question I'd expected. Better the tongue of a serpent than a thankless lover. 'It seemed stuitably presidential,' I told her. 'Besides, I'm not paying for it.'

'My word,' Laurie said, 'I should think not.' She was lying with her hands behind her head, and the light from the bedside lamp backlit the line of her face against the pillow. Relaxed, without those glasses, she looked about twenty. Well, why not? She wouldn't be thirty for a couple of years yet. For me, forty loomed.

She said, 'Tell me about the boy who pinched the car.'

I said, 'He's a lovely man, to be sure. A stage Irishman with a compulsion to drive Rolls.'

'Don't most joy-riders?'

'Curiously,' I told her, 'they don't. There are plenty of people who want to *own* a Rolls. The status symbol bit. But it's not the kind of car joy-riders seem to fancy. They go for a spin in any old Porsche or Ferrari that's lying around, but a Rolls doesn't seem to do much for them.'

'So what makes Mr Miller different?'

I said, 'No reason. It's just that his knowledge is oddly patchy. There doesn't seem to be a thing he doesn't know about which model is which and when they were made, but technically he hasn't a clue.'

Laurie frowned. 'So? Just because you like a certain car doesn't mean you have to know how it works.'

'Well, no. But he pretends he does.' I remembered how Miller had been so forthcoming about the output of the various engines, notwithstanding the fact that Rolls have always been excessively coy about revealing relevant figures. Nasty-natured people hitched their cars up to dynometers and found out for themselves. I knew roughly the kind of figures they got, and in no way did they tie up with the ones Miller had quoted.

Laurie frowned. 'So what does that make him?'

'You know,' I said, 'I bought my first clapped-out old banger when I was eighteen and I've never been without a car since. Yet the Maserati's the only one I've had stolen. Which is funny when you come to think of it.'

'Not funny,' Laurie said. 'Lucky.'

'All right,' I conceded. 'Lucky. But it is funny that a couple of days later the same thing happens again.'

Laurie yawned. 'Darling, you're making a thing about it. It was Gus's Rolls that got taken, not yours. And it was taken by a boy called Miller, not your murderous Ginger.'

'So?'

'So there's nothing *significant* about the two incidents. It's just coincidence.'

'You may be interested to know,' I said, 'that the Rogues' secretary has a photograph pinned up of himself in happy mercenary days. Got a few pals of his with him, too, all loaded down with grenades, machine pistols, the lot. There was one with black hair who looked familiar although I couldn't quite place him. But I've just remembered something.' I paused in order to give my punch line a chance.

'And?'

I said, 'I remembered the chap's build all right, it was just the black hair that threw me. But of course in monochrome film the tone that prints blackest isn't black—it's red. The man in the picture talking to Blunt was Ginger. How's that for a coincidence?'

CHAPTER 8

'Of course you must go,' Adrian Todhunter said. 'Really, Straun, I'm surprised at you.'

I said, 'The President hardly needs protection in his own country. I'd just be going for the ride.' Through the window behind Todhunter's head a Foreign Office pigeon observed us with ill-concealed impatience. Perhaps he got fed when they were alone.

Todhunter joined the tips of his fingers together and stared at them to see if they fitted. He said petulantly, 'I should have thought you would have enjoyed the experience. We have great hopes of Chakra. If we hadn't, we shouldn't have gone to the trouble of seconding you in the first place. But seeing that H.E. seems to enjoy your company, it would be highly embarrassing if we suddenly had to say you weren't available. And a good deal worse if we told him you simply didn't want to go.' He stopped studying his fingers and looked up. '*Why* don't you want to go? Has the President offended you in some way?'

'No,' I said, 'he's a pleasant enough chap.'

'So?'

I wondered briefly whether to tell him about the bullet through my golf bag but if I didn't know where it had come from it seemed unlikely Todhunter would do better.

'Look,' I said, 'during the past week two car thefts and a murder have taken place under my nose. As I'm a policeman and not a bloody travel courier, I think it's high time I got back to work.'

'I spoke to your people about that.' Todhunter turned his head and looked out of his window. Possibly he was looking for his pigeon but it wasn't there. 'They said all

three incidents are in the hands of the appropriate depart-
ments and they're quite happy about your continued
secondment.'

Thank you, Chief Inspector Gareth Evans. 'No comment,' I said.

'Now tell me the real reason you don't want to go.' He
had a certain perception, had Todhunter.

Well, why? 'Put it down to my fey Scots blood,' I told
him.

'Bad vibes?' Todhunter prided himself on his command
of the modern idiom.

I stood up and prepared for off. 'Let's say if things go on
as they are, there'll be tears before bedtime. But I'm not
sure for who.'

I went out into the pale sunshine and took a taxi to
Bacton Street. Tiverton House looked its usual nineteen-
thirties ferro-concrete self, my grey mistress, suddenly
almost dear to me. Sergeant Endicott was at lunch, come
to that almost everyone was at lunch. I looked at my in-tray
in the hope that it would offer some kind of reprieve, but it
didn't, so I rang my insurance broker. If Peter Rankin was
at lunch too it would serve me right for making private calls
in the firm's time, but he was at his desk so maybe it was
all right.

'I have yet to see an estimate for your little bit of trouble,'
he greeted me.

'Still waiting for it.' Peter as yet was unaware of the
extent of my little bit of trouble, so I went on hurriedly. 'I
wanted to have a word about this renewal notice,' I told
him. This was no time to have any slip-ups about cover.
'Am I right in thinking there are a few noughts too many?'
It was a conversation which we had in similar vein every
year, and merely underlined the inescapable fact that
insuring exotic Italian sports cars is an expensive business.
That I managed to remain constantly surprised was

because each year the figure managed to be almost ludicrously higher than the last.

'No mistake, I'm afraid.' Rankin's voice in my ear
sounded philosopical, understandably, as he was collecting
the money, not paying it.

I said, 'But it's monstrous.'

'Then let me get you fixed up with a restricted use policy.
Say four thousand miles a year. You'll save a packet.'

I said, 'But I do a hell of a lot more than four thousand.'

'I know you do. Keep the Maserati for high days
and holidays and get a Metro or something for running
around.'

'There's no point in owning a decent car and keeping it
locked up in a garage.' I felt rather like a small boy stamping his foot but we'd been through all this before. I said,
'Statistically, a classic car has got to be a better risk than
a rep's hatchback. A man who's driving company transport
doesn't really worry whether he wraps it round a tree or not,
whereas he'll take damn good care of his own investment.'

I could imagine Rankin raising his eyes to Heaven but
his voice was patient. 'All right, so this discerning owner of
yours seldom exceeds forty miles an hour. He never even
scratches his precious car. But he can *lose* it, for God's sake!
I've got a claim on my desk at this moment for a Khamsin—it's even the same colour as yours. Stolen last week
from a garage in Bayswater and it'll cost the company thirty
grand. Do you still wonder that premiums are high?'

'Whose was it?' There weren't that many Khamsins in
the country and I knew most of them.

'Bill Deacon's'. Probably a breach of confidence but
Rankin was aware that I knew Bill.

I said, 'But Deacon doesn't own a Khamsin, he's bought
a Ghibli.' Maseratis tend to be named after exotic winds
but I could never picture a Ghibli as anything other than
a kind of rodent.

'He *used* to have a Ghibli,' Rankin corrected me. 'He'd swapped it only last week.'

I said vaguely, 'I must have forgotten. When did you say he lost it?'

I could hear him shuffling paper. 'The twelfth. Why?'

'It was the day after someone tried to steal mine.' It was the day they'd found Oscar. It was the day Paddy had said Oscar had been out in Deacon's car.

'Was it? Was it?' Not sympathetic but interested. 'I suppose someone wanted it.'

'Obviously.'

'I mean, someone must have ordered a red Khamsin. The buggers steal cars to order these days, don't they? Probably have them on computer or something.'

'Something like that.'

'You'd like to think about cutting down on your mileage?'

'No,' I said, 'leave it as it is. I'll send you a cheque.'

'Just as you please, old man. But you're wasting money.'

I put the phone down and sat looking at it. I don't know why I felt so surprised but I'd never had much to do with stolen cars. Like any other large organization, the police force is departmentalized and nothing overlaps all that much. Really, I knew very little more about the gentle art of the car thief than the next man. Probably less than my insurance broker. I went downstairs to General Branch and asked about it.

'Birkin,' someone said. 'Sergeant Dave Birkin's "Stolen Vehicles".'

'Just Birkin?'

'He's the one who knows what it's about, sir.'

I took his word for it. Birkin lived in the garage sub-basement and it was the first time I'd visited the place. I'd imagined, supposing that I'd thought about it at all, that it would be wall to wall patrol cars, but these were appar-

ently next door. What confronted me in fact was wall to
wall motorcycles, leavened with the odd car. Fluorescent
ceiling tubes highlighted the dust and mud, making the
place look like an acre of junk, although presumably each
vehicle had once been desirable enough for someone to steal
it. Now they had been recovered and were awaiting claim in
a kind of mechanical dogs' home while a broad-shouldered,
no-nonsense-looking sergeant in well pressed blue dunga-
rees crouched beside a big Kawasaki, whistling tunelessly.
I hovered and introduced myself, reluctant to break his
train of thought, there being times when expertise takes
precedence over rank.

'I'm Dave Birkin. They told me you were coming.' He
didn't look up, but his concentration made it no dis-
courtesy.

I said sourly, 'News gets around.'

He grinned and straightened his back. 'I was just getting
ready to open a special file for you. Even Inspectors don't
lose Maseratis every day.'

'Well,' I told him, 'now you won't have to. I've got the
car back. What's left of it.'

He nodded. 'Sorry it was like that. There are countries
where thieves have their hands cut off. I can't help thinking
it might be a good idea if we had the same arrangement
here.' I wondered if he'd have done the job himself. Looking
at Birkin, he struck you first as good-looking in a toughish,
rugger club kind of way, then secondly as something else.
But what?

I said, 'You sound as though you meant that.'

'Oh, I do. I happen to like cars.'

Well so did I, but enough's enough. I said, 'I just wanted
to pick your brains for a few minutes.' I wanted to pick his
brains very badly, because if there was any truth in folklore
this sergeant of 'A' Division knew more about stolen
vehicles than any computer in the country.

'OK.' Birkin glanced down at something that resembled a strip of chewing gum gripped in his fingers. 'Hell—'

I made sympathetic noises.

'It's a Synprint.' He held up his treasure for me to see. It still looked like chewing gum, but with faint markings embedded in it. He gestured towards the frame of the Kawasaki. 'First thing the bastards do is chisel off the frame number. Sometimes you can stick this stuff over it and it'll bring up the original number well enough to read, but they worked hard on this one.'

'So what do we do now?'

He shrugged his shoulders. 'One can try with ultra-violet light but it's not all that good.' He paused. 'I remember your car well. KFT 590X. Red. Cream upholstery. The ex-Lord Dorne car. You bought it through Peregrine Motors last year.'

'That's the one.' Well, he could have mugged it up, but impressive just the same. I said, 'If my car hadn't been piled up I suppose it would have gone straight to a port and never been seen in this country again?'

Sergeant Birkin smiled faintly. 'It's a chance, of course. But we'd hope to do better than let them get away with that!'

'So how would you stop them?'

Birkin said shortly, 'He'd have to wait hours for a crossing, because the first car ferry this morning was at 1015 hours, Dover to Zeebrugge. We'd have had all usable ports alerted and waiting for him by that time.'

'What's a usable port?'

'One that fits in with the thief's time-scale. I'll show you.' The sergeant led the way to his office, a glassed-off chunk of the basement, surprisingly clean and orderly, businesslike apart from a photograph of a remarkably pretty girl. 'Here.' He went over to a large-scale map of the South of England that covered about half the available wall and swung a pointing finger round the capital in a wide circle. 'Available time.'

'Between the snatch and the ferry.'

'Correct.'

I looked from the map to Birkin. 'Suppose,' I said, 'you take me through a representative incident.'

'Of course, sir.' I wondered why I qualified for a 'sir' now and not before. Birkin added, 'You choose the car.'

Well there was no point in having it too close to home. I said, 'BMW.'

'What series?'

'Seven.'

'Quite collectable.' Birkin nodded approvingly. He was an enthusiast all right. He went on, 'The owner's a senior partner in a firm of rather trendy accountants with clients in the media. The order's for a grey car, with a manual box.'

'So someone actually makes an order for a specific make and type?'

'Oh yes,' Birkin said. 'It's a business, after all. Surely you don't think they take just anything that comes along?'

To tell the truth I hadn't thought about it at all very much, and who were 'they' anyway? But I just nodded.

'There were 465,000 cars nicked in Britain last year,' Birkin informed me. 'Nearly half a million. Most of the jobs were semi-amateur, of course, and what we're dealing with here is the true professional.'

'Who does what?'

'The driver—the thief—the villain—first has to find his car. Right make, right year, type, whatever. He identifies the owner.' Birkin corrected himself. 'Well, not down to name, because the owner's name is not important, whereas his routine is. If the car's parked outside an office all week, does it just stand there from ten till five or is it used? If it's outside a house, is it left there all night? It's up to the operator to keep his eyes open until he knows a time-band that is safe. A period when he can be reasonably sure the car isn't in use.' He glanced round at me. 'Shall we say, for the sake of argument, that our BMW is always unattended between the hours of 0930 and 1230?'

I nodded agreement.

'So our driver knows that if he nicks his car at 0930 the chances are that he's got three clear hours before anyone even notices that it's gone.'

'If he's lucky,' I said.

'So he's unlucky now and then,' Sergeant Birkin said shortly. 'If he wants a quiet life he works in an insurance office.'

'All right,' I agreed. 'He's got three hours.' Experts, I knew from experience, were notoriously touchy about interruptions.

'He'll know exactly how far he can drive in three hours,' Birkin said. '*Exactly* how far. And without going so fast that he draws attention to himself. So he draws a circle on his map accordingly. At whatever port lies within the circle he books a crossing for himself and his car. Nine times out of ten, by the time the car's reported missing it's already out of the country.'

I said, 'What happens if there doesn't happen to be a port within three hours' driving?'

'He just has to nick a car that is.'

'So what about documentation?'

'No problem. The thief just fills it up as required. All he has to do is write down the car's description—you don't have to prove ownership to book a ferry.'

That sounded like asking for trouble but I didn't make the rules and I didn't want to break in on Birkin. The man obviously knew a lot about car theft and I was anxious to learn. I said, 'The system really works?'

Birkin laughed. 'Believe me, sir, it works for *anything!*
These operators shift dumpers, JCBs, cranes—they even
ship articulated lorry cabs out two at a time, back to back
in a container!'

Containers were big. I said, 'You could take several cars
at once that way.'

'Too right!' Birkin agreed. 'In this business the boys are
brilliant at packing. *Brilliant.* Last week we lost two Volvo
300 Turbos—you know, the cab end of a 35-tonner artic?
They'd got them both in a single container—one of them
upside down so that they packed in neatly. They stuff containers full of stolen bulldozers and ship them off to the
Middle East where they can never get enough. In Dubai
they'll take as much earth-moving equipment as you can
supply and no questions asked, and the Baltic States aren't
all that fussy about cranes, either.'

I asked, 'How the devil do you hide a crane?'

'In a box, same as everything else.' Birkin looked surprised. 'Oh, I know they *look* big, but they come to pieces.
They're only like a big Meccano model, after all.'

'So if you're a contractor out there you can actually place
an order for what you want?'

Birkin shook his head doubtfully. 'You'd probably have
to take what was available in the heavy equipment line, but
cars, yes. If you've got the right contacts you can get just
about any car you want, down to the colour.'

'Where do they go?' I asked him. 'I mean, what's the
best market for prestige cars?'

'You're looking at a country that's short of cash,' Birkin
said. 'Short of foreign currency, that is. If there's no foreign
currency then there's nothing to buy expensive foreign toys
and there are always people who want them. Politicians
mostly. The wheelers and dealers who've got Swiss bank
accounts and don't mean to go short.'

'Which means?'

'Oh, Africa,' Birkin said. 'No two ways about it. Africa every bloody time.'

I found a chair and sat down. 'What part of Africa?'

'Well, there's a big market in Northern Kentola. Lots of money up top and no pounds or dollars.' Birkin considered that market for a moment. 'They say the government car park there is something to see. Ferraris, Rollers—the lot. And every last one's been borrowed from somebody.'

'From this country?'

'So far as I know.'

'But why just us?'

'Probably,' Birkin said, 'because this particular operation has got a corner in the African market.'

'But why is stealing cars so popular in this country? Damn it, the place is an island! Why not pinch cars from Holland, for instance?'

'Every country has car thieves.' Birkin liked being asked questions. If you know the answers, who doesn't? 'The picture is different, that's all. In Italy, for instance, they seem to prefer the part to the whole. Leave your car outside a restaurant and when you come out the car will still be there, only it won't have any wheels. You mention Holland. Well, the Dutch are a practical people. The police there drive Porsche 911s but everyone else trundles around in Golfs and small Merc diesels. Basically it all boils down to tax.'

'Tax?'

Birkin corrected himself. 'Well, tax and chauvinism. In most European countries people choose to drive their own national cars. Italians drive Fiats, Germans Mercedes and VWs, French Citroëns and Peugeots. Maybe it's not patriotism—it's possible they just *like* their own cars. But in England it's different. We love buying foreign cars and won't say a good word for our own. And then the tax system comes in. European firms don't buy their employees cars, whereas here the company car is a cherished perk. Top men are allowed to choose what they want, and they have educated tastes, so if you want a spread of quality cars regardless of nationality, the UK is the place to go.' Birkin shrugged his shoulders. 'So someone is making a fortune.'

Well, there was always someone making a fortune somewhere. 'But if there's no foreign currency,' I said, 'how does the seller collect? Or does he just take it out in coffee?'

'You'd have to have a word with the finance boys about that,' Birkin conceded. 'It's complicated. The short answer is that your average bent politician has his money salted away in a Swiss bank account and he buys his shiny new car out of that. Of course we're talking about very poor countries where there isn't much money about, what with international aid being given in kind and all that sort of thing, but you'd be surprised what a cash flow there is, just the same.'

I asked, 'What about foreign nationals? If I managed to collect the price of the car on the spot, could I bring it home?'

'No, you couldn't.' Sergeant Birkin had no doubts about that. 'And anyway, if you managed to smuggle out all that local currency nobody would want to change it for you on the outside. But then again, my friends tell me there are always ways.'

I said, 'I bet there are. Tell me one.'

'Of course one gets out of date,' Birkin said apologetically. 'But I know there used to be a thriving business in one African country that shall be nameless. The Whites were still running their farms there, and while most of them had plenty of money in the bank they couldn't transfer it out of the country. It was frustrating for them, because it meant they couldn't get out themselves unless they left their piggy banks behind.'

'Very frustrating,' I agreed. 'So what did they do?'

'They bought light aircraft. Some not so light, either.

Then they flew the things out and sold them. So much flying capital, you might say.'

I could see snags, like where the aircraft came from in the first place, but nobody thanks you for lousing up a good story and anyway, like Birkin said, if you really want the ins and outs then go to the experts. Birkin knew cars, not money.

'Physically,' I said, 'how do the cars get there? Presumably they're not delivered by road.' I tried to imagine some exotic Italian confection leaping from one elephant dropping to the next. Not on.

'How do they get to Kentola?' Birkin looked regretful. 'If anyone is knowing, they're not talking. The airport's been staked out for months, likewise the roads through South Africa. And don't tell me they come in by sea because Kentola doesn't have a coast.'

We looked at each other. All experts need someone to feed them their lines now and again and I wasn't one to let him down. 'But you've got a hunch,' I said.

Birkin looked pleased. 'Oh, they get in through Chakra,' he said. 'No doubt about it. But I'm damned if I know how.'

CHAPTER 9

'*So you're going to Africa*—' Sir Charles Brown, heading across the living-room of his Kelvington Mews place, glass in hand to back up the smoking jacket and black tie. Unlike anyone else I'd ever met, Charlie Brown could wear a maroon velvet smoking jacket and somehow contrive not to look absurd in it while he hosted half-a-dozen people for a homely snack. I was talking to nice Alice Brown, looking as wholesome as a girl can in six or seven hundred pounds' worth of little black dress, and who somehow contrived to appear impressed at the news.

'Are you really! Oh, you are lucky! I've never been to Africa.' Well, maybe she hadn't though she must have been most everywhere else, but you still believed her. She must have been about fifty, and the kind of older woman every right-thinking young man dreams of being seduced by. Certainly one didn't have to use much imagination to guess at the sensational creature she must have been thirty years back. I think she felt the same way herself because she had a weakness for 'sixties clothes and music and cars, the whole Beatles scene down to the furnishing of the house. It struck me sometimes that the whole thing was slightly sad, as though it was vital that her surroundings stay for ever the way they'd been when she was a girl. Misplaced sympathy when one considered the fact that her doting husband indulged Alice to the extent of giving her an immaculately restored white Jaguar XK 120, which must have been worth a king's ransom.

'For God's sake, Charlie!' I'd protested at the time. 'Alice can't use a car like that for shopping!'

Charlie had said cheerfully, 'I don't see why not. I use

a Brough Superior when we're out at the country place. Machinery's meant to be used. No point in keeping it in museums.'

I'd tried to picture Sir Charles on the brass and copper monster that used to be called 'the Rolls-Royce of motor-cycles' and gave up. Charlie Brown on two wheels at a hundred miles an hour didn't bear thinking about, but I did, now and again. With envy, I suppose.

'Angus, how's your drink?' Charlie arrived at my side and exchanged with Alice one of those private husband-and-wife signals that seem to consist of some kind of telepathy and Alice pushed off, which left Charlie free to take me on one side.

'Chakra, I hear.' He'd forgotten he'd asked me about my drink.

'Yes,' I said, 'that's right. Just a short trip.'

Charlie Brown said abruptly, 'Did you know Kentola's full of stolen cars?'

If he was trying to make me jump, he very nearly suc-ceeded, but fortunately not quite. 'Not my section,' I told him guardedly. 'But, yes, I've heard something about it.'

'Do we—you—know how they get there?'

'No,' I told him, 'I don't.' Dead right I didn't.

Charlie swirled ice around his glass. 'The popular theory seems to be that they get in via Chakra. That *I* organize it in some way.' He looked at me narrowly. 'I'm not asking if you've heard this bit. Maybe you have, maybe you haven't. But your chaps are highly suspicious of the Chakra relief plans I've been organizing. They're supposed to be landing agricultural gear and mine-drilling equipment. Now certain people are saying that some of the pilots are also carrying the odd car.'

Certain people. Which certain people? I sat there and did my best to look slightly interested, politely concerned, whereas it was all I could do to restrain myself from running round in circles and foaming at the mouth. I had no delusions that this was some kind of coincidence, that I just happened to be going to Chakra and Charlie Brown just happened to be under some kind of surveillance. Did I see in all this the machinations of Adrian Todhunter, or did I have to thank Special Branch? One thing I did know was that I shouldn't find out anything by asking.

'It's the first I've heard about it,' I said, and spoke no more than the truth.

'Check it out while you're over there,' Charlie said. 'So far as I'm concerned, I can make money without flogging stolen cars, but I suppose it's just possible the odd crew are running a little something on the side. So maybe you could check a few arrivals? See if anyone's coming in unscheduled? That kind of thing.'

This wasn't what I'd expected. 'Look,' I said, 'I'm going over there to keep the President company while he plays golf. I don't imagine there'll be much time to nose about airfields.'

'I understand.' Charlie put on his understanding face. 'Just if you get the chance. I'd count it a favour.'

'*So you're going to Africa*—' Sergeant Endicott clearing my Out-tray and not filling up the In as a sign that he personally had got the message.

'Correct, Sergeant Endicott,' I agreed. 'Any objections?'

'You take care of yourself, sir. Africa's not like London.'

'I'll do that.' Endicott's family home was Jamaica. He'd never personally set foot in Africa but he had his prejudices, like everyone else.

'Does Sergeant Birkin know?' Endicott was doing his West Indian looking unconcerned act, which wasn't unconcerned at all.

'If he does,' I said, 'he hasn't got it from me. But he doesn't strike me as a chap who misses much.'

Endicott rearranged his papers preparatory to taking them away. 'He doesn't miss anything at *all*.'

'I should hope not indeed.' I caught his disapproving eye and added, 'The man's a walking computer, with a quite exceptional record. Do I gather that you're personally not over fond of him?'

Endicott shrugged his shoulders. 'So if he's gay, he's gay. No law against it.'

Well, no. But why had my sergeant spotted something that I had not? I said, 'What makes you so sure he's homosexual?'

Endicott frowned. 'I played squash with him a few times.'

I had a quick memory of Joe Endicott's startlingly beautiful wife. It was hard not to laugh. 'You mean,' I said, 'that he propositioned you?'

'No *sir!*' Endicott looked shocked.

'Then how do you know?'

'I just know, sir.' The stubborn look that I'd learnt to recognize had come down over his eyes. There were certain things that Sergeant Joe liked to play pretty close to his chest and apparently this was one of them. In the early days of our association I'd tried to pressure him into sharing them but had come up against a blank wall. In time I'd get around to accepting the fact that in some areas the West Indian is a good deal more finely tuned than his Anglo-Saxon counterpart. There didn't have to be any overt suggestions or whatever, but if Joe had a hunch that Birkin was gay then I believed him.

'Well,' I said, 'if you say so. But he's got a picture of a very presentable girl on his desk and I don't imagine it's his sister.'

'Could be he's AC-DC.'

'Could be.' But logically a bisexual would have a picture of each or none at all. And anyway, what did it matter?

Birkin's private life was his own, and a good thing too. I shook my head at Endicott. 'Forget it.'

He nodded woodenly. 'Yes, sir. Forget it.'

'So you're going to Africa—' Yes, Laurie, my love, I am going to Africa and leaving you behind. Well, you were invited but you turned it down. Because you had a job to do. Because you had a job to do if nobody else had, which was what you inferred.

In the dark she said, 'It's not a policeman's job. You know that.'

'I know.' There was no moon but the reflected lights of middle of the night London threw a kind of glow on to the bed, tinting her fair hair pink. 'I know,' I said, 'but orders is orders. If you're sent, you go.'

'You don't know what you're letting yourself in for.'

I turned over and looked at her. She was looking at me, too. I said, 'I'm not sure what I'm letting myself in for either, come to that. But I can't very well turn the job down.'

'Turn the whole damn thing down. You can earn a living writing. You don't have to be a policeman.'

In our early days it had been Laurie who had soft-pedalled the idea of writing for a living. What had happened to make her change her mind?

I said, 'I don't mind being a policeman.' Which was male-speak for I rather liked it. 'I just don't like being hired out. Particularly on jobs I don't understand. It's conceivable that a Third World president wants a golfing bodyguard. It's reasonable that he seems to use golf as tourist bait. But the car bit I don't understand.'

'You said yourself you shouldn't have left your car outside.'

'So Oscar gets killed. Gus's car gets nicked. Someone tries to shoot Gus—'

'That could have been an accident. There was that shooting ground right next door.'

'Yes,' I said, 'it could have been an accident. And it could be coincidence that Gus's country is a channel for stolen cars. But if you believe that, you'll believe anything.'

'So what do you want to do?'

'Given the chance,' I said, 'I think I'd like to go back on the beat.'

She laughed softly. One of the good times, to lie in bed and listen to one's girl laughing in the dark. 'Now?'

'No,' I said, 'not right now. I have other ideas for right now.'

CHAPTER 10

Eleven hours is at least ten hours too long to spend in an aircraft, but the flight between London and Kentola could have been worse. It could have been a lot worse. A glimpse, while boarding, of the battery rows of Economy passengers reminded me just how awful it would have been if I hadn't been travelling First Class on His Excellency's money. Well, somebody's money. A twinge of Calvinistic guilt, one of the occupational hazards of being my kind of Scot. But really, no great sin in being comfortable and being civil to the pleasant uniformed lass who seemed to want to dripfeed me champagne (not my favourite drink), so I was stone cold sober as I stumbled shivering down the steps into the pre-dawn chill. Mist lay low on the ground and small service vehicles crept in and out of it like mice. Within the terminal, groups of exotically garbed travellers huddled around the stationery carousel. Most of them looked as though they'd never tried anything more technical than tending sheep, but they had the same air of resigned cynicism that marks the air traveller wheresoe'er he be. I wandered across to the windows that faced inland. Lined up on the far side of the approach road the antique Peugeot and Citroën taxis drooped disconsolately in sympathy with their owners. Faced with the same total ban on imported vehicles, Indians and Pakistanis cheered things up with elaborate paintwork, but evidently in Kentola the thing to do was to sit back and watch the thing decay. I wondered who maintained them and how. With his back to me, a middle-aged African in a well-cut linen suit waved to some-one. For a moment I imagined he was wanting a taxi but instead a silver-grey car nosed out of the adjacent car park and came to a standstill in front of him. A 7 series BMW, chauffeur-driven. I watched its owner climb in the back and start to open his briefcase as the car moved away, its place being taken by an immaculate black Mercedes 300 which made its collection and gave way to a similar model in white. Pick-up time. Taken all round, it was a show that made the trip worthwhile and I wished David Birkin could have been beside me to enjoy it. Apart from anything else, Birkin could probably have told me which of those cars had been stolen and which not. If any. Indeed, if any. If Kentola wasn't importing cars it meant that with the exception of the odd visitor the whole lot were illegal. How many CD plates had there been? Hard to see from inside the building, perhaps two. Which left—how many? A dozen. Twenty. I'd lost count. I wondered how their proud owners managed to run the things so openly without anyone asking questions. But then, who'd ask the questions? Anyone with enough clout to query the boys I'd been watching would be in on the racket himself. Interesting, though.

I picked up my bags and joined a cheerfully haphazard mob around the information desk in the hope of finding my connection to Chakra. Someone had brought a goat which was eating everything in sight. It was a shambles, but as an airport it worked better than most. A big gentleman in shirtsleeves pointed me in the direction of a Fokker Friendship and I got myself aboard without the goat but alongside a plump lady clutching a Bible. I wondered if it was missionary zeal or simply a distrust of planes. If the latter, we had a good deal in common, but she started reading the moment we got off the ground so it seemed no moment to intrude and I looked out of the window instead.

Funny old country. I was no old Africa hand, a few trips here and there, six months once in Kenya, more than enough. People said the place called you back, which it didn't, so far as I was concerned, and maybe it needed more time. It was bloody big, I'd say that for it. The ramshackle outskirts of the town fell back and when next I looked there was only a great stretch of red dust, a dirt road, scattered villages here and there. Flying low, as we were, there wasn't much one could see. A few cow-like creatures swerved uneasily as the shadow of the aircraft touched them. Out on the horizon, low hills loomed in a blue-grey haze. What must it have been like to walk across this land on foot?

Someone in the seat behind me said, 'Well, I've been out here thirteen years without learning the language and I'm damned if I'm going to start now . . .'

Beneath us the hills had come up, scrub-covered and as near desert as made no difference. The plane lurched as the pilot throttled back and the flaps came down. If I ducked my head I could just make out the edge of the capital, and further on again the thin blue line of the sea. We landed in a cloud of dust and taxied up to the airport building, which someone had constructed with more enthusiasm than sense, complete with a message in letters two feet high: CHAKRA WELCOMES YOU.

Well, that was nice.

I emerged unscathed from the cheerfully haphazard passport control ('We all hopes you have a great time!'), looked out of the windows of the terminal and took in the modest airfield with its single runway. I could see the 40-seater Friendship I'd just left and an aged Dakota, but that was the lot. Hard to imagine the place could have taken anything much bigger, but I checked.

'What you see's about it, man. We ain't got no big airport.' Harassed, like all officials, but helpful.

I said, 'But you get international relief supplies?'

My informant nodded. 'Just small stuff, in Friendships. Never could take the big loads, machinery and such. That always hauled in by road.'

Well, Charlie Brown had asked me to check and I'd

checked. Nobody yet had ever stuffed a car into a Fokker Friendship or anything like it. Peanuts was in the clear. I went through the doors and outside Birdie O'Shea pushed his way out of the crowd to greet me.

'It's grand to see you, Mr Straun, sir! It's been a long time.' It had and, though he'd lost some of the old Oirish, nobody would seriously think he came from anywhere else.

'Good to see you again, Birdie.' We shook hands. To be honest, I'd have passed him in the street without recognizing him. Big, fair-haired, with an open, deceptively innocent face and a way of walking that reminded one of an out of uniform soldier.

All in all, a bit out of character for a golfer, but then, how often had I met him? Twice, maybe three times, on different sides of a very big fence, and small-time crooks tend to look much alike anyway. Only, of course, Birdie O'Shea wasn't a small-time crook any more, he was a highly respected designer of golf courses. Thanks to me, I suppose. An odd thought.

We stood and looked at each other for a moment. I suppose it wasn't the easiest meeting in the world for either of us; the past is best left there, and perhaps while we were thinking that a porter was picking up my gear and the moment had gone and we were walking out to the car.

Not a car, in fact, but a green Suzuki 4 × 4 with *Panorama Golf Construction* emblazoned on the side. Birdie got in behind the wheel. He said, 'If it were no for some foreign ambassador or such, ye'd have had the President himself to meet you, so you would.'

President Welcomes Golfing Policeman. Good headline stuff. I said, 'Perhaps it's just as well he couldn't make it.' I was glancing up and down the dusty airport road, but wherever Britain's finest stolen cars were going it certainly wasn't here. Morris Oxfords, Ford Prefects, a few unidentifiable

Hillmans—a curious sensation of being back in the 'fifties. Most people seemed to be getting about on cycles, which was probably a sensible thing to do.

'President Gus is a fine gentleman.' Birdie drove at the cycles and let them cope as best they could. He glanced at me sideways. 'You'll have played a round with him?'

'A few holes,' I said.

Birdie nodded. 'Man, he's no idea.'

I said, 'I know. But he's fond of the game.'

'Aye.' Birdie laughed, unexpectedly. 'He's a lovely man, to be sure.' He swung the wheel to avoid hitting a donkey. 'We'd best go to your hotel first.'

'Yes,' I said, 'I'd like that.' I meant it, because it must have been in the eighties and I was wearing an ordinary British suit. I sat back and let the hot wind blow over me. The airfield was three or four miles outside the capital and I looked out curiously over the dusty countryside as the Suzuki bounced merrily from pothole to pothole. But there were crops in the fields and the brightly dressed local women looked cheerful enough. The villages had that curiously ramshackle look peculiar to urban Africa, an uneasy transition from one culture to another through the medium of corrugated iron. It was scruffy and not all that pretty but it was a long way from the hopeless-looking places one sees on news reports. Many a tourist paradise had been profitably manufactured out of less.

After a few miles we turned off the road into the driveway of the kind of architectural extravagance they do rather well in Florida, apart from the fact that the Americans do it for fun and this was for real. White, half Moorish, half Byzantine, with palm trees about the door.

Birdie must have noticed my expression. 'Aye,' he said, 'it's the hotel. It used to be the President's palace. The last President, you'll understand.'

I saw that there'd been some changes made. No wonder

the new regime was going down well. I asked where the top man lived now.

'In a bungalow near the Legislature.' Birdie sounded approving, which I suppose was a not untypical outsider's reaction to frugality on the part of an administration out of which he'd made a great deal of money. He added, 'The President does most of his entertaining at the Clubhouse. You're due there at seven, by the way.'

'Seven. I'll remember.'

'That'll be after visiting Mr Brainbridge at *The Post*. You'll have heard of Mr Brainbridge?'

I said no, I hadn't.

'He runs the local newspaper.' Birdie corrected himself. 'He *owns* the thing. They say it's one of the oldest English-language papers in Africa.'

'That's nice,' I said. 'And that's why I have to see him?'

'Sure an' you must be joking, Mr Straun! You'll be seeing the man because he's secretary of the Golf Club.'

Well, I could see his point. 'All right,' I said. Nobody wants to get on the wrong side of the club secretary.

Birdie looked relieved. 'That's fine, then. Now you'll be getting yourself settled in an' I'll fetch a caddy car.' He paused. 'You'll be wanting to look at the course?'

Well, I supposed so. Why else was I here? I said, 'Whenever you're ready.'

The hotel was empty but splendid in a slightly odd way. I had a shower and changed into drill slacks and a bush shirt. From the bedroom window one could see the ups and downs of a golf course stretching out towards a heat-misty horizon. I went downstairs to find Birdie O'Shea waiting for me with one of those engaging little vehicles with which Americans enable fatties to cover enormous courses in double-quick time.

'You're ready, sor?'

'It's ready I am,' I said. It was catching.

I climbed aboard. We were alongside the first tee and I stared through the windscreen at Kinto Park. Six thousand, four hundred and seventy-one yards, Par 72. From where I sat it wasn't anything spectacular, but it wasn't by any means bad. Golf courses that flourish in Asia and the Middle East often have a parched look that even a monsoon cannot really dismiss, but this didn't look unlike a similar project in Europe caught at the same moment of development. It was a bit flat, the small lake that formed a water hazard was obviously artificial, and the raised greens showed scarred faces where the bulldozers rented from Zimbabwe had shoved the earth up, but what the hell, a year in that climate and nobody would know the difference.

I asked Birdie how long the job had taken, and he said six months.

'From scratch?' Six months for laying out the basics was believable but this place was ready to play.

Birdie grinned. 'Aye!' Then, when he saw that I didn't believe him, he got out and kicked the fairway with his heel. 'Sand down there. It's like building one of those old links courses. Grand drainage, it is.' He climbed back beside me and we drove slowly down the deserted fairways while he gave me a blow-by-blow account of how he'd made each one. Golf course construction is a specialized business that demands the skills of architect, professional golfer and civil engineer. I did remember that one of the doyens of the craft had said something to the effect that economy in course construction consisted of getting the best for the least, without too much involvement in what Americans loosely call 'moving dirt'. Just driving over it made it clear that the President's brainchild was no state of the art confection calculated to make a tour professional pull out all the stops just to go round in level par. The short holes were not over-bunkered, so that an averagely good player could have reasonable hopes of making a birdie, the long ones reachable in two by top people but comfortably in three by anyone else. To me it seemed eminently sensible as a course, offering eighteen sound, enjoyable holes for the typical club player, no more, no less. It would never be a championship course, but then, who was going to want to play a championship on it?

'How much is all this costing?' I asked. On the face of it that was none of my business but I could imagine that sooner or later some politician would try and make a name for himself by wanting to know how it was a poverty-stricken Third World country could afford, of all things, a golf course.

Was the new government in Chakra getting its priorities right? Was not golf elitist? Was not golf an unfortunate reminder of our shameful imperial past?

'A fair wee bit.' Birdie was not letting me into any State secrets. 'But there's a lot of labour costs in building a golf course, a terrible lot of labour, and as we know well enough, the President's fond of a game himself. If it hadn't been for himself, all this would still be scrub or mealie meal or whatever Godforsaken crop was here before. As it is, he's provided a grand lot of workmen, and it's not cost us a penny. I was after bringing three or four of my own lads out to oversee, but they've long gone. All in all, it's been a fine cost-effective operation.'

I said, 'So you had just about a free hand.'

'I'd not be saying that.' Birdie looked genuinely regretful.

'So what is it you can't have?'

He thought it over. For a moment I think he genuinely had doubts about telling me. Perhaps he thought a professional ambition was too private a nonsense to share, but in the end he changed his mind. 'You'll be knowing the seventeenth at Sawgrass?'

'I've never played anywhere in Florida.' Then I remembered that it was hardly necessary to play Sawgrass personally in order to have at least a nodding acquaintance with one of the most photographed holes in the world. It's short, and the green's a little island, surrounded by a hundred yards of bright blue lake. You chip across the water, and if you're clever enough to put enough back spin on your ball to make it stay on, you follow it up by means of a little causeway. I said, 'Oh, that one.'

'Yes,' Birdie said, 'that one.' He nodded through the windscreen. 'This is the seventh course I've been making. Seven! And each time I think what a grand thing it'd be if I could have an island hole. It's a daft fancy, but it can get to be an obsession with a man, so it can.'

I said, 'Well, why don't you make one, then?'

Birdie gave me the kind of look one reserves for children who ask tiresome questions. 'Now, how can I be insisting? I can design it in well enough, but I'm not after paying the bills.'

I said sympathetically, 'And every time they make you take it out.'

'They do that.'

Well, I could see their point. An island hole wouldn't be on anyway, except in the tropics, unless the course included a large lake. Besides which, a feature that may be fun for a professional could be a nightmare for a long handicapper to whom every less than perfect drive meant a ball lost in the water. I said tentatively, 'What about here?'

Birdie sighed. He'd not struck me as a man given to sighing, but we all have our weaknesses. 'Man,' he said, 'you should see it.'

'You mean,' I said, 'it's a natural?'

'As natural as God made it. Just a bit beyond the thirteenth.' He swung the wheel over and we headed for the line of tree-covered high ground that, according to my rather elementary sense of direction, should overlook the sea. The ground beneath the trees was sandy but the Suzuki ploughed up easily enough on four-wheel drive. Once on top I could see that a twenty-foot swathe through the trees had been cut and levelled. We lurched along it for a hundred yards and then ground to a stop.

'Sure,' Birdie said, 'and that's a fine thing for a man to see!'

It was a fine thing to see all right. Below us, a beach of silver sand stretched as far as the eye could reach. Beyond it the sea was like blue glass, and a hundred yards from the shore a tiny island glowed like an emerald in the sun. Twenty-five yards wide at the most, it was more a large rock than an island, but you'd have had to be blind not to see it as Birdie O'Shea's dream come true. The Good Lord had even made the thing flat and caused something green to grow on it.

I said, 'It would make a wonderful photograph.' We don't all have the same enthusiasms, and as a potential hole I gave it about four out of ten. But it was true that here was the potential for a hole people would talk about when they got home. And it would look great on the travel brochures. I looked at Birdie. 'Doesn't the President like the idea?'

'The President's a lovely man. He likes it well enough.'

'So what's the problem?'

Birdie said with disgust, 'Now what would it be but the old story, Mr Straun? Bloody politics.' He waved at the bank on which we stood. 'The Ridge is an army training area, an' you'll be knowing what that means. Then there's some kind of wee tribal minority who've got a claim, to say nothing of the odd laddie who'd like fine to turn the place into another Costa Brava—'

'So what's the President doing about it?' Gus hadn't struck me as the kind of Chief Executive who'd allow people to get in the way of his golf, but one never knew.

'The man's no fool,' Birdie said grimly, 'but he's new and he's not going to step on the army's feet. Besides, there's the Committee. If the Committee says it'll not be having an island hole, that's all there is to it.'

I rather liked the idea of the President of a country being at the mercy of the Committee of his own golf club. A lot of men in his position would simply have shot the more difficult members and co-opted people who shared his views on golf course design.

Birdie said abruptly, 'I'm away to have a leak.' He turned away and tramped down the slope and disappeared behind a convenient tree. I turned my back on him and studied the island and what had once been a beer barrel, half swallowed up by the sand. Some kind of seabird dropped down on the barrel, a white, gull-type creature with a yellow beak and bright button eyes. We regarded each other amiably, not being each other's prey. Apart from the faint lapping of the sea it was astonishingly quiet.

'Hi, bird!' I said.

The bird looked at me. I must have been the last thing he ever saw because a heavy machine-gun opened up some-where pretty close and dissolved him into red mush, lowered its trajectory a mite and blew the barrel apart. At my feet the sand boiled as several hundred rounds a minute ploughed into it.

I dropped and rolled and the bullet storm followed me.

CHAPTER 11

I've a hard head and by the time I'd ended flat on my back, six feet down the slope, I knew what was happening all right. Over the years most people have the odd little moment when Uncle Fred trips with a cocked rifle in his hands or some maniac looses off on the other side of the valley, and you duck to the once-heard-never-to-be-forgotten whirr of a bullet in flight. Just one bullet, mind you. Not this.

The first burst from the machine-gun had demolished the barrel. Now whoever was firing the thing was blasting a few feet over the top of where it had been and I lay rigid, listening to that hellish cacophony of torn air above me as six hundred rounds a minute hosed out to sea. Logic told me I was safe enough just so long as I stayed where I was. The army had training courses where happy warriors crawled under barbed wire entanglements with fixed-line machine-guns blasting away over the top of them into the bargain. I hadn't even barbed wire, so what was I worrying about? I was worrying because I knew that these guns weren't on fixed lines, and that whereas army instructors don't actively try to kill their men, I was not personally in the army. As someone once observed, policemen are open season any old time.

The firing stopped.

I stayed where I was and thought things over. Maybe I was on an army training area but even so a few thousand rounds from a heavy machine-gun straight at me seemed slightly over the top. And where was Birdie? My friend Birdie was supposedly coyly relieving himself behind a tree, which was almost laughably convenient. *I won't be a minute. Just going to have a leak* . . . Had he known? *Had* he known?

I got up on my hands and knees. There was still silence, apart from the wind in the trees and the gentle paddle-pool sound of the sea. Then someone shouted, to be answered by other shouts. Apart from the shredded barrel and a few red scraps of flesh and feathers, everything looked much as it had before. There were voices amid the trees on the landward side and I wondered what would be the sensible thing to do. If I ran, I'd be a sitting duck. On the other hand, I was reluctant to give whoever it was the satisfaction of finding me grovelling on my hands and knees.

'Oh well,' I said aloud and climbed up on to my feet at the same moment that Birdie O'Shea came out from the trees and headed for the combat-rigged local soldiery as though he was one of Butcher Blunt's mercenaries in full cry.

'Is it bloody mad you are!' he was shouting. 'A friend of the President, and—' He caught sight of me and stopped dead. 'God save us! Is it all right you are?'

'And where were you,' I inquired, 'when the lights went out?' I didn't bother to make it sound friendly because that wasn't the way I was feeling.

Birdie looked hurt. 'Sure an' I was behind a tree when I heard a sound like World War Three starting. I nipped back—'

A tough young officer said, 'Sorry. It was a mistake.'

Behind him, a dozen or so equally tough-looking soldiery, one of them with a belt of machine gun-ammunition looped round his neck. They were all armed with semi-automatic rifles, they were all studying me with the kind of detached interest well-trained troops assume when faced with someone they may be ordered to kill at any minute.

I said, 'The mistake being that you missed me?'

The army consulted with itself in what was presumably Shosi and someone got busy with a pack radio. Movement on the part of Birdie or myself seemed unwise, judging by the amount of weaponry that pointed our way when we tried it, so we stood and admired the view until eventually a jeep came batting along the beach and disgorged a tallish officer in a red-tabbed combat jacket. He came up from the beach at an easy lope and saluted.

'I am General Tombi.' A good-looking officer in the late thirty age bracket, high cheekbones, concerned eyes. 'You'll be Mr Straun.' His voice sounded as though it still missed Sandhurst.

'I still am,' I said. 'Just.'

The General smiled faintly. 'Sorry about that. You've no idea the trouble there'd have been if we'd accidentally hit you.'

'You mean,' I said, 'you *weren't* trying to hit us?' Us? Me? Either by luck or good judgement my good friend Birdie had been well out of the firing line.

General Tombi looked amused at the idea. 'Good Lord, no! These chaps aren't allowed to shoot *people*! That was their mark, out there.' He pointed out to sea where, beyond the little island, something bobbed in the blue water. I narrowed my eyes against the glare. Some kind of barrel, with a marker flag. Probably a similar barrel to the one the unfortunate bird had sat on. But well, yes— a target.

'All right, General,' I said. 'No harm done.'

'Call me Joe. Everyone calls me Joe.'

I bet the chaps standing respectfully in the background didn't.

I said, 'No harm done, Joe.'

General Joe looked relieved. 'So glad. Birdie been showing you round the course?'

I nodded. 'Do you play?'

'No. There are other things to do.' He looked reflectively
at his troops. 'Where do you go next?'

Birdie answered for me. 'We're due at *The Post* at six. He
hasn't met Mr Brainbridge yet.'

'Second-generation editor, been out here thirty years.
Secretary to the Golf Club, too.' The General glanced at
his watch. 'Time these chaps knocked off for the day anyway. Only do more damage. Besides, I'd like to come with
you.'

He came with us. We'd been due at the newspaper office
at six and in the event we were five minutes early, but that
didn't seem to matter, because Brainbridge was at the door,
all affability, doing the welcoming bit. A shaggy, grey-
haired character with hornrimmed glasses and the air of a
seedy academic, although his offices were rather impressive:
a low, brick-built complex with iron fencing and a dozen
cars in the park beside the main door. There was a larger
building tied on behind, which I guessed held the printing
plant. The ground beneath my feet vibrated slightly and
there was a low hum as a background, so I guessed that
the presses were running.

Brainbridge said, 'My dear Straun, my name is Brainbridge.' He said it heartily, like a parson who hasn't
seen one of his flock in church lately. 'I've been looking
forward to meeting you. Did you have a good afternoon?'

'It was one hell of an afternoon,' Birdie told him. 'There
were troops exercising and they let fly at him with a
machine-gun.'

'You can't be serious!' Brainbridge and O'Shea exchanged the kind of glance that co-patriots keep for such
moments in a foreign country, the report of the latest
uncouthness of their hosts. *Have you heard what they have done
now?* Race memories of this massacre and that atrocity.

Well, this wasn't Surbiton, that was for sure, but nobody asked them to come.

I said, 'We were where we shouldn't have been. Apologies all round. No harm done.'

'You wouldn't have been saying that if you hadn't ducked bloody quick,' Birdie said.

Well, he had a point. I remembered what those chunks of metal had sounded like, going overhead. 'Oh well,' I said, 'I did, so let's forget it.'

Brainbridge said fussily, 'It's no laughing matter. Still, come along. I'll show you round. We'll start in the news room.'

He led the way inside. Birdie stayed where he was. Why not? He'd handed me over and I didn't imagine he was particularly interested in how the local newspaper worked. Had he really set me up back there? I tried to assess the probabilities. What could there have been in it for him? Precious little, I'd have thought. Maybe I was getting a shade too touchy.

'Well, here we are,' Brainbridge said.

I looked around. I was no newspaperman but it wasn't the first news room I'd been into, though in this form I guessed it would probably be the last. Not a direct print-in terminal in sight. Half a dozen chaps in shirtsleeves sitting at cluttered desks dominated by ancient steam typewriters. A large notice with foot-high letters pinned to the wall said SUB YOUR COPY FIRST! Retired Fleet Street hacks would have wept nostalgic tears at the sight.

'Sam Tamba, our News Editor,' Brainbridge said in my ear.

'Hi!' said the News Editor who, apart from the fact that he was black, must have looked much like any other News Editor one was likely to see, tough, preoccupied, on top of his job.

'I was just showing Mr Straun around,' Brainbridge said.
He was Editor in Chief and owner of the paper but he
didn't want trouble.

'Sure,' Sam Tamba said. 'You go ahead.' He wore an
eyeshade, in the manner of his kind in vintage Hollywood
films.

I said something about *The Post* being the country's
largest-selling paper. The News Editor grinned. 'Man, it's
the country's *only* paper.'

I looked at Brainbridge. 'So you're the voice of Chakra.'

He didn't smile. 'One tends to be the voice of the
government.'

I asked, 'What happens if you don't agree with the
government?'

This time he did smile. 'My dear Straun, one has to be
realistic. Independence has a fine ring to it but it doesn't
pay the bills.'

I'm not sure what I'd have said to that but someone
called Brainbridge to a phone a couple of desks away and
after a few moments he waved to Tamba to join him.
Together they pored over a galley proof, leaving me standing by the News Editor's desk. I looked around with the
vaguely self-conscious air of a non-mixer abandoned in the
middle of a party, noting that Sam Tamba used an ancient
Lexicon 80 typewriter and, judging by his ashtray, had a
workable source of Camel cigarettes. At one side of his desk
was a sheaf of typescripts and proofs impaled on a kind of
metal hook and I wondered why it was familiar. The penny
dropped. A spike. *I spiked his story*. Curiously, it hadn't
occurred to me that the traditional fate of unwanted items
was, in fact, a real spike. I wondered what happened to
those over-late bits of news at the end of the day. Did
anyone ever look at them again or did some office boy
simply pull them all off and chuck them in the waste-bin?
I stared idly at the last item to be rejected. Curiosity has

killed a great deal more people than the cat. I reached out and unfolded the pierced sheet and read the headline that hadn't made it.

TRAGIC ACCIDENT ON GOLF COURSE
VISITING POLICEMAN SHOT DEAD.

CHAPTER 12

If Gus Aligar had issued invitation cards he could have
headed them AN EVENING WITH THE PRESIDENT, the kind of
cosy get-together of the chosen that only needed an
unobtrusive television camera stuck in a corner to make the
whole thing disturbingly familiar. Borrow from one
another's culture if one must, but why do we always pick
the awful bits? Maybe his decision to entertain us at the
new golf clubhouse didn't help. There are clubhouses and
clubhouses, and although some are distinctly odd it's an
oddness that has grown up over the years as a temporary
shack gets a bit tacked on here and there and maybe rates
real bricks and a coat of paint whenever the club can afford
it. Gus's brainchild looked as though he'd studied photographs of half the clubhouses in England and tried to
capture the spirit of all in one. He hadn't succeeded, of
course. It had clapboarding, it had shutters. There was a
little tower with a clock on it. There was a verandah. Well,
why not? He'd got the place going, that was the main thing.

'Angus, so glad you could come!' Kiki wearing a flame
full-length dress that clung to her like a wet-suit on a diver.
She'd pulled her blue-black hair straight back off her fore-
head and suspended what looked like four or five ounces of
diamond from each ear. Effectively, she wore no jewellery
on her dress, but those incredible fingers were weighted
down with rings like knuckledusters. She'd looked good in
sports clothes; in social gear she was sensational.

'Real glad!' The President was beside her, less obtrusive
in a white dinner jacket and a red bow tie but still not
exactly someone you'd miss. He looked amiable and relaxed
and if he resented being number two-ed by his lady he was

taking care not to show it. 'Great to see you again, Angus. What do you think of the clubhouse? Isn't it something?'

'Yes,' I agreed. 'It certainly is.'

'You reckon visitors will like it?'

I said, 'They'll like it all right.'

'Great!' Gus looked relieved. 'You fixed up OK?'

'Just great!' I said.

'You know these folks?'

I looked them over. It's a strange feeling studying a roomful of people and wondering how many of them had been looking forward to reading of my demise in the next day's paper. *Reports of my death have been greatly exaggerated.* Who'd said that? I prodded around in my memory but singularly without success. So who had we got? Robert (spiked any good stories lately?) Brainbridge and Monica, his mousey wife. A tough-looking young colonel plus Birdie O'Shea, resplendent in a green dinner jacket.

'For God's sake, Birdie! You won the Masters?'

He looked hurt. Maybe he actually liked the thing. 'Och, it's just showing the flag. They like that sort of thing here.'

The small, round black man with hornrimmed glasses would be Emmanuel Bosoto, Opposition Leader. There was an odd lady of middle years in a native *jeallaba* who, when the President did the necessary, turned out to be a Ms Megan Wishart. Ms Wishart said, 'This must be a novel exprience for you, Mr Straun.'

Well, yes. Like rising from the dead? Adrian Todhunter was a great believer in keeping tabs on long-term British ex-pats in sensitive areas on the premise that all information comes in useful sooner or later. He'd shown me the file on Brainbridge and Megan Wishart, which had been interesting but innocuous. Now I could see that the press clipping photographs had made a fair job of her but they hadn't captured that curious transparent skin quality that so often goes with ladies who run health food shops. According to her CV,

Ms Wishart had started life as a missionary's daughter before drifting into revolutionary politics, a couple of fringe religions and thence to African social history. She'd spent most of her life in one part of Africa or another and was at present the more or less self-appointed guardian of Chakra's ethnic heritage. Unkindly, one might say she had a bee in her bonnet, but by all accounts a pretty well informed bee. Even so, she didn't have to be patronizing. Novel experience, indeed.

'Oh, I don't know,' I said. 'One gets invited into all kinds of places to mind the silver.'

She gave me a look that wasn't as Christian as it might have been but left it at that. Kiki smiled faintly and raised an eyebrow, Robert Brainbridge scowled, and put his hand on my arm. He said with some ill grace, 'You know we're having a committee meeting this evening?'

I hadn't known. 'Here?'

He said impatiently, 'The clubhouse isn't ready yet so this will have to do. Incidentally, you're co-opted.'

'Any particular reason?' Committees were something I normally avoided like the plague.

Brainbridge shrugged. 'God knows. Orders from on high.'

He made it absolutely clear that this was a presidential whim with which he did not agree.

'All right,' I said reluctantly. 'I'll serve.'

We milled around for a bit and a steward in a white coat brought suitably frosted drinks for the ladies and beer in silver tankards for the chaps. After a while Gus called us into the Committee Room and we settled down at the long table with an agenda neatly laid out in front of each chair. I looked mine over with a certain amount of curiosity.

*Meeting of the Committee of Kinto Park Golf Club Tuesday
November 11th.*

If you've seen one agenda you've seen the lot, but it was
the first time I'd sat in on a golf club committee meeting
in foreign parts. A let-down really, since it was as little
different as research could make it. President Gus in the
chair as Captain; Robert Brainbridge, Secretary; Colonel
Ram, Treasurer; Kiki, Ladies' Captain. Birdie appeared to
be the Greens Committee, which was understandable in
view of the fact that he was probably the only one who
knew anything about the subject along with Mr Bosoto,
and I sat in as directed.

'Minutes of the last meeting—' the President was saying.
He sat back while Brainbridge read them out, apparently
a record of the inaugural get-together. Name, objects, fund-
ing, election of officers. To be fair, Gus handled it all
remarkably well, being new to the job and there being a
fairish difference between being President of a country and
boss man of a small golf club. Or so I imagined, never
having tried either job. I listened to Brainbridge droning
on and found myself watching the other members. I wondered how many of them, apart from Gus and Kiki, actually
played golf. Colonel Ram probably. But Megan Wishart?
Bosoto? What would they say if I asked them to have a
game? And which ladies was Kiki going to captain?

'Is it your wish that I sign these minutes?'

The usual mumble of 'Ayes', pencils raised. Weird, the
whole thing. If they didn't play golf, why join the club?
Because it was the 'in' thing to do? Well, not unreasonable
in a small community, when you came to think of it. Most
clubs carried their quota of non-playing social members,
although they certainly didn't sit on the main committee.
I tried to call to mind the other Europeans I'd seen since
my arrival. Precious few. By all accounts there were a number of foremen and supervisors at the copper mines at

Tando and Neirie and presumably a fairish number in or
around the capital. But they'd be the tough, skilled artisans
who kept a certain type of overseas project running, and I
suspected Gus's idea of a club was something along the
lines of an African Wentworth. Somebody, sooner or later,
was going to have to explain to him that founding a good
golf club wasn't primarily a business of class distinction.
And anyway, what good is a club with only a handful of
members?

I went on listening without much enthusiasm, other
people's domestic problems being a good deal less than
riveting, quite apart from the fact that the club was too new
to be involved in anything much apart from membership
fees, opening hours of the clubhouse bar, when they got a
clubhouse, the kind of food available therein, and whether
visitors should be asked to produce a handicap certificate.
Where had Brainbridge dug that one up, I wondered? The
readers' letters column of *Golf World?*

'Item Six. Report on condition of greens. Mr O'Shea.'

Mr O'Shea reported, rather impressively I thought. He
knew his drainage and his root mixes and was apparently
deeply into reinforcing tricky bits with a new kind of plastic
mesh. Considering the fact that he was acting not only as
golf professional, head greenkeeper and a kind of resident
course architect into the bargain, I thought he was doing
remarkably well, backed up with a team of local grounds-
men to whom the idea of tending grass at all must have
come as something of a novelty. God knows how much of
it made sense to his audience. I'd always understood that
plastic mesh strengthening was designed to protect municipal courses from extra heavy use, which I should have
thought was just about the last thing the Kinto Club would
have to worry about, but nobody raised a query. Perhaps
Birdie was just having them on. Or perhaps they were
having Birdie on.

He said abruptly, 'An' while we're on the subject of
greens, I'd like to be raising the matter of the thirteenth.'

Oh, he would, would he? I started to pay attention.
Nobody else was apparently pricking up their ears but there
is a moment in any discussion when someone comes out
with a key phrase that announces that the preliminaries are
over and the main bout of the evening is about to begin.
Megan Wishart was nibbling the end of her pencil, Brainbridge doodling something on his agenda paper, the others
looking slightly bored.

Gus said politely, 'Yes, Mr O'Shea?'

'I thought we'd agreed that there was no point in discussing The Ridge.' Megan Wishart had put her pencil
down and was fixing Birdie with those pale and unfriendly
eyes.

Gus looked at her. 'Nevertheless the matter has been
raised.'

'But—'

'And it is customary to address the meeting through the
Chair.'

Ms Wishart went pink. 'Sorry, Mr Chairman.'

'Just to keep the record straight.' I had to admire the
man. He could have been a good retired half-colonel knocking the local tradesmen's heads together. *I know you're not
gentlemen but it will make things so much easier if we pretend you
are*—Pause, then again, 'Mr O'Shea?'

Birdie was in no way put off and after all he talked like
he breathed, what Irishman doesn't? 'You've got a fair
enough course for a fair enough price, Mr Chairman, but
let's be honest now, it's not by way of being one that your
guests will be remembering. A parkland eighteen holes an'
none the worse for that. But who's to deny that we've got
the makings of a world class hole on our doorstep. Extend
the Twelfth, an' take in a bit of The Ridge so we can be
using that wee island for the thirteenth green. With the

colour of that water an' your white sand, there'll be pho-
tographers coming here in droves.'

Gus rubbed his chin. 'I agree, Mr O'Shea. It would be
a dramatic hole. Unfortunately, The Ridge is not part of
the land allocated for the golf course.'

'I'm well aware o' that. But it could be.' In moments of
stress Birdie was not inhibited by rank.

Gus said, 'Sure, no trouble. But you're not going to get
everyone to go along with you, you know that. You've got
the Golf Club committee here, and even *they* won't back
you.'

I half-expected Birdie to object, but he didn't. I suppose
he knew it was true. Gus sighed and looked at the Colonel.
'Ram, how does the army feel about us having that bit of
The Ridge for an extra hole?'

I watched the young colonel look apologetic. 'Mr
Chairman, we've already taken this up with General
Tombi. He's very much against breaking up a training
area for the sake of a golf course. Apparently there are a
number of factors involved—' A British officer's voice,
regretfully explaining why even a President can't fight
City Hall.

'Sure, I understand.' Gus looked towards Megan Wishart. 'You wanted to make a point earlier. Maybe we could
hear it now.'

Megan Wishart said, 'Of course we can't touch that part
of The Ridge. You know that.'

'Maybe we could have it again for the benefit of Mr
Straun?'

'It's a tribal section.' She was looking at me defensively
as though at any moment I might pose a direct threat to
her tribes. 'It's a sacred area. A vital part of the Tebi
culture, time out of mind.'

Well, she would know, but I wondered if I was the
only one who found it odd to have a white woman

doing the fronting for a black culture. I asked, 'In what
way?'

'They hold religious ceremonies there.'

'All the time?'

'Dark of the moon,' Gus said unexpectedly. 'Once a
month.'

La Wishart gave him the kind of look wives generally
reserve for husbands who speak out of turn and I wondered
why. But like all enthusiasts, she probably found it genuinely offensive for anyone else to voice an opinion on a
subject that was her own preserve. I could imagine her
asking just how much the President knew about his own
people when he'd spent most of his life in the United States.
Tribal customs they may have in Manhattan, but they are
not the same as the ones back home.

She repeated flatly, 'The place has been a vital part of
the Tebi culture time out of mind.'

Gus was looking resigned. Having spent most of his life
around New York, I rather doubted if he knew much about
tribal culture anyway. He turned to Emmanuel Bosoto.
'You know any Tebis?'

Emmanuel Bosoto cleared his throat. 'I am a Tebi.'

Well, I hadn't actually imagined he was going to look
any different from anyone else, so why be surprised? Had
the others known? Of course the others had known!

'So you, personally, would object if we extended the golf
course to include part of The Ridge?'

Bosoto was a politician, and straight answers didn't come
naturally to him but he didn't see a way out of this one.
'Yes,' he said, 'I would.'

'And so far as you know, other members of your tribe
would object too?'

'Yes.'

'And you'd back their views in Parliament?'

Embarrassed silence. For a moment I thought Bosoto

was going to tell his President to mind his own business but, give him his due, he didn't. He said, 'I'm not sure the question is in order, but the answer is yes.'

'Mr Straun?' My turn, though nothing to do with me.

'Well, you've got the makings of a great hole,' I said. 'You don't have to do much because it's natural, so all you've got to do is grow some decent grass on it. You'll have something that'll photograph like a million dollars. The local objections aren't anything to do with me.'

We all looked at each other.

'We are at the mercy,' Robert Brainbridge announced finally, 'of the bloody ethnic lobby.'

If he intended that as a good, flat, unanswerable statement, it didn't do him much good. 'If it hadn't been for the bloody ethnic lobby,' Megan Wishart told him crisply, 'you'd have been building time-share bungalows on the place by now.'

Would he indeed? I waited for more but it wasn't forthcoming, but Gus really had very little to learn about chairing a committee. 'Maybe we should have a show of hands?'

We had a show of hands. Gus didn't vote and Birdie couldn't, and it was unanimous against. Gus nodded to Brainbridge to make the necessary record, then turned to our end of the table. 'Sorry, Birdie. One hole we'll have to do without, I guess.'

Birdie shrugged. 'Aye. We'll be managing as best we can.'

'Any other business?'

There was no other business.

'Time for a few drinks before dinner, then.'

We had the few drinks on the verandah overlooking the course, dinner in the panelled dining-room with reproduction Spy cartoons on the walls. I suppose it was Gus's idea of an English clubhouse, and in a way it was, though the food was a good deal better. I thought of Harlington's frozen scampi and chips, with a mixed grill on Saturday night. No wonder Gus liked The Rogues.

Birdie said watchfully, 'It's a fine thirst they're having.'

A fine thirst indeed, not that he was doing too badly himself. I don't know where the champagne came from, Bollinger 1972, presumably part of the late lamented incumbent's ill-gotten stocks. The food was good, served capably by white-jacketed stewards. President Gus, his lady, Birdie and I talked golf, the others of this and that. I suppressed an urge to ask one of them who they reckoned was going to win the Open, then changed my mind. There was unlikely to be a law of the land that said members of a golf club had to be interested in the game. After all, they'd say, it was only like a livery company. How many Cordwainers could wain cord?

It was an odd party. It has to be an odd party when a committee dines alone in a clubhouse that's otherwise empty because there are no members. Even odder when one knows that some or all of that committee expected you to be dead some hours ago.

I leaned against the bar and drank cautiously. Outside the windows, night had come down like a blanket. The dark of the moon. I wondered what the Tebi tribe would be doing, or if indeed they would be doing anything. Extraordinary how the founder members of a golf club could manage to find so many different reasons for not improving their course. The army I could understand best because armies everywhere have an insatiable appetite for land over which they can play war games, and politics were politics the world over. Megan Wishart was a classic do-gooder with a proven track record to back her up, and if Robert Brainbridge wasn't planning a fortune out of development, somebody else soon would. All different reasons. All to the same end.

'Win some, lose some.' The President put a consoling arm round my shoulder. 'Come into the next room. Kiki's going to sing.'

Oh God, I thought, it's going to be one of those evenings. Laurie had been right, I shouldn't have come. But I did as I was told and the President's lady seated herself at a rather nice piano and sang St James Infirmary Blues.

She wasn't bad. Like most of her race, she had a natural musical talent and an inborn affinity with the blues, and her voice had the harsh spikiness of an old gramophone record. But for me, that was about it. She was a black girl singing the blues, but if she'd been a white girl singing Cole Porter nobody would have fought to sign her up. On the other hand, Kiki was undoubtedly something to look at. She caught my eye unhurriedly and I felt as though I'd taken hold of a couple of terminals wired direct to the mains. Well, that was just another of Gus's local problems, I thought, and one that I could do without. She had switched from blues and was trying her luck with an old Nellie Lucher number and I signalled a steward and got myself another drink. It had all the makings of a long, hard night.

It was about midnight when I walked back home to the hotel, still open for me, it's only guest. From the window of my room I could see part of the course by starlight, but not much. I took off my light-coloured linen suit and put on navy slacks, rubber-soled golf shoes and a black roll-necked sweater. Then I turned out the light and went downstairs by way of the fire escape.

By my reckoning it was about a mile to The Ridge if I crossed the course by the most direct way, and I set off at a brisk jogging trot, slowing to a walk when something large and dark loomed ahead. The Professional's shop. The Club with a Committee and no members, yet with a shop already comfortably full of gear. Someone would have to explain about first things first. But then, flogging equipment to non-players might in the long term be a good idea. A shadow darker than the rest moved. Gus's voice said, 'Going somewhere, man?'

CHAPTER 13

I stopped. Gus materialized beside me. A black man on a dark night is hard to see at the best of times and his clothes were as dark as mine. I said, 'A little exercise to clear the head.'

'Well, yes. I guess we need it.' He was as sober as I was. How useful that art of appearing to drink while not. 'How about a few holes?'

'In the dark?'

I saw his teeth as he smiled. 'You mean you've never got with illuminated balls?'

Bill Loakes, back at Harlington, had been captain that year and had chosen to play himself in at midnight with the help of trick balls. It had been odd, watching the bright green projectile arcing across the sky and then bouncing merrily up the fairway. A gimmick, sure enough, but at least one had been able to find the damn thing. 'I've seen them,' I told him. 'Never played with one.'

'Some in the shop. I got the key.'

He opened the door and switched on the light. I wondered how long he'd been waiting for me. Come to that, if there was anyone else out there. Gus tossed me a pack of three balls. 'There you go.'

I took them from him and inspected the things. They were green and translucent, dimpled like an ordinary ball but with a plug recessed into the cover that concealed a stick of some kind of slow-burning chemical. Once lit, according to the blurb on the carton, the ball would glow for about three hours and have the same playing characteristics as a regular ball.

'Very clever.' I handed them back to their proud owner. 'What about clubs?'

'No sweat. Birdie laid on sets to rent.'

We helped ourselves to a half set apiece and an electric trolley. Leaves stirred, clattering loudly in the wind, and the air was suddenly full of small sounds.

Gus frowned. 'Rain coming.'

'Now?'

'Hell, I don't know. Never know in these places. But soon, I guess.'

There was something essentially eerie about the whole business, anyway. How had Gus known I was planning to walk up to The Ridge? And supposing I didn't go along with midnight golf? I guessed that he'd have a gun on him somewhere, which was more than I had, not wishing to have trouble with African Customs. But if he was really determined to make sure I didn't go poking around the local beach, why fool around playing games?

I looked at the sky. With no moon it was hard to tell whether there were clouds or not, but the stars still seemed to be there. We went out to the first tee, while Gus fiddled with the balls and eventually got them going. They glowed with an intense green light, rather eerie, really.

I said, 'All right. Off you go.'

His Excellency the President stuck a tee in the ground, mounted his king-sized firefly on it and gave it a smack. It was a good drive, quite spectacular, a tiny, bright green sphere shooting off like a mini-satellite across the sky, swooping down on the dark fairway, a big bounce, a smaller bounce, bump bump bump.

'Good shot,' I said, and meant it, but then we had a good British tradition of the condemned man tipping the executioner. Playing golf in the middle of the night was a new skill so far as I was concerned, so it was not easy to judge just how good it was. Still, it was straight as a die and if time in the air was anything to go by, two hundred-odd yards. A good hit. A quite remarkably good hit for someone who'd drunk as much as he had. There are a few formidable individuals who seem to be able to drink and drive with a certain amount of accuracy, but the only ones I'd met had been professionals who could almost certainly have beaten Gus if they'd played blindfold. Ergo, my friend the President either played a much better game than he pretended, which wasn't likely, or he wasn't as tight as he was pretending to be, which was.

'There's nothing to it,' President Gus said. 'Try your luck.' Agin nature, as they say. Oh well. I gave it a clout and made good contact. I don't exactly know what I expected but it felt just like any other golf ball and, so far as one could judge, it went just as far. Topped it a fraction but it ran on low, scampering along the dark fairway like some kind of demented will-o'-the wisp. Finally it caught up with my opponent's effort and the two balls sat there side by side, looking rather like the eyes of some monstrous creature of the night. Well, at least you could see the damn things, I thought, I gave them that. I could name a few courses where they'd have been a boon in daylight, let alone in the middle of the night.

'Hell,' Gus said, 'this is fun. You want to have a pound or so on the side?'

'My father warned me about playing with people who made suggestions like that, particularly if I couldn't see what I was aiming at.'

'Same for both. You chicken or somethin'?' Either the man was schizoid or he really thought this was a normal game. Oh well, if he could do it, so could I.

I said, 'You can bet your life I'm chicken. But we'll have a quid a hole if you like.'

'I do like,' Gus told me. 'This country's not so prosperous it can turn down easy money from the West.' He marched off into the dark. With only a ball to steer by, so to speak, it was an odd experience.

One does some odd things when one's tight, so I suppose playing a game of golf in the dark wasn't unreasonable. Apart from the fact that I suspected my partner was sober and I knew that I was. So who was fooling who? I didn't know, but we got along the course somehow, the President rather the better of the two, having played it before. I think I enjoyed putting the most, if enjoy is the word, the curious fascination of watching that bright green ball running across the green towards the flag and then suddenly vanishing as it dropped into the hole. We made a local rule about keeping the flag in. Come to that, we made a number of local rules as we went along, some kind of latitude seeming permissible in the circumstances. Where the holes included hazards such as areas of scrub thorn, we missed them out altogether, enough being something of enough; likewise the longer holes that struck out into the wilds and seemed likely to involve a lot of walking back. Which was probably the reason we ended up on the short thirteenth, with The Ridge standing high and clear between us and the sea. We sat down beside it, and the air was full of the wind in the trees and the distant lap of water.

Gus looked up. 'What say we play onto the island? Likely to be the only chance we'll ever get.'

It was late and I was edgy. I said, 'Look, supposing we stop playing silly buggers. There's no moon. The Ridge is out of bounds. What's more, you know *why* it's out of bounds. So why pretend we're here to play golf?'

Gus prodded the grass with the heel of the club he was holding. 'For Chrissake, Angus, I don't know any more than you do.'

'Then why were you out here waiting for me?'

'I wasn't waiting for you. Just coincidence we both planned on doing the same thing, I guess.' Gus sounded more amused than embarrassed. He apparently had no difficulty in guessing what I was going to say next, because he added, 'OK, so we both know it wasn't golf. That was kind of the first thing that came into my head.'

'You were making a trip to The Ridge, too,' I said.

The President nodded. 'Sure. Weren't you?'

'Yes,' I replied. 'Now you tell me why you were going.'

Gus smiled disarmingly. One thing about a black man smiling in the dark, you can always see it. He said, 'Hell, no reason. Just that with everyone being so damn sure the place was off limits, I got curious.'

'You never got curious before?'

'I never got anyone to be curious *with* before.'

I said, 'It's late already, Mr President.'

'Gus.'

I said, 'In words of one syllable, Gus, what the bloody hell do you think you're going to find up on The Ridge tonight?'

He thought that one over. Finally: 'I know damn well what *you* think you're going to find. You think you're going to find a container ship unloading stolen European cars like there's no tomorrow. Inspector Straun solves mystery of Kentola's top car racket!' Gus beat time with his club head in the dust. 'No way. Nearest place you could bring any kind of boat inshore is a coupla hundred miles north of here. Water's too shallow. Whatever anyone does up there, I tell you it ain't got nothin' to do with cars.'

That odd little flutter of wind stirred again and at the back of it there was something that wasn't wind, but a steady beating of drums. We must both have heard it but neither of us made any comment. 'All right,' I said, 'let's forget the cars. Let's just go and see if either of us can hit one of these damn silly balls on to that island.'

Gus got to his feet. 'Now you're making sense.'

I wasn't making any kind of sense, but then it was getting

to be that kind of night. But I picked up my clubs and together we trudged to the top of The Ridge. Curiously, it was darker there than it had been further inland.

'It's cloud coming up over the sea,' Gus said when I pointed it out to him. 'No starlight.'

'Can't even see the island.' I stood staring into the gloom and after a while my eyes got used to it and I could just make out the triangular scrap of land where it stuck up out of the water, eighty yards or so offshore. We were out of our minds, but since we were here, it seemed a pity not to get on with it. I said, 'Where do we drive from, anyway?'

Gus prodded the ground with his toe. 'Here, I guess. About where the tee would be if there was one.' He dropped a bright green ball and selected a club. 'What do you think? Eight iron?'

I was listening to the background beat of the drums, which seemed to be getting a good deal louder, and wishing I was somewhere else. How in God's name had I got myself into this? I said, 'Listen—'

But Gus didn't want to listen, he had just swung his iron and the bright green star at his feet flew up in a great arc across the night sky, plummeted down and landed almost exactly in the shadowy centre of the island. As a kind of celestial applause, there came a distant rumble of thunder.

'Eight iron,' he said. 'Spot on.'

I said, 'Nice shot,' and picked up my own club. My mind could hardly have been less on the job but I knew I'd feel a fool if I missed. I stared out towards Gus's ball glowing at me in the distance, and in that moment the storm broke and a jagged fork of lightning stabbed down blue-white towards the horizon. It seemed so near, so frighteningly vivid, that it was one with the tearing rasp of thunder that crashed out over our heads. Rain, like a waterfall, smashed down on top of us, lightning jumped and flickered like some giant's flashgun, throwing up trees and the beach and the

island beyond in harsh contrast, like a Victorian stereo-
scopic postcard. I stood there frozen by the shock of the
thing, but as I stared out over the lagoon it wasn't the
island that riveted my attention. What held me spellbound
was the sight of a red Maserati being driven across the sea
towards the shore.

CHAPTER 14

How long does a flash of lightning last? Not long. Even the crackling, flickering discharge of a tropical storm that seems to go on for ever can't extend much beyond a couple of seconds, but in that time there wasn't much I missed. Back-lit by the storm, the car looked so real you could have reached out and touched it. And why not? The damn thing was real enough. Simple logic decreed that you couldn't drive a car over water, but then, we live in an inventive age.

I stood timeless in the bucketing rain and then the moment was over and the lightning was gone and there I was, back in the middle of a night as black as the pit, with rain running down my face and my retinas in a state of shock. The echoes of the thunderclap had died away but the drumming hadn't, if anything it was even louder than before. There's something compelling about almost anything deeply rhythmical, and perversely, the less one understands it the harder you have to listen.

'Enough is enough,' Gus was saying. 'Let's make for home.'

I said, 'Did you see the car?'

'What car?'

I said, 'Forget it.' The unseen drummer had reached the bit he always seemed to find hard. Odd how the stuff grew on one. Behind me, Gus was still asking about cars but I ignored him. It was hellishly dark but every now and then a faint splutter of lightning lit the top of The Ridge enough for me to see the track and I started to run along it. Run to the sound of the drums. Who had said that? Nobody actually, someone said something like it. I pounded on like a maniac, trusting that the next flash would keep me on course. Wet palm fronds slapped at me and the sandy path grew heavy with water. Running through drenched trees with the lightning going on and off like giant strobe lights was like fleeing from something in a nightmare. Part of me knew well enough that I was crazy to be getting myself mixed up in this, while the other half seemed conscious of nothing save a need to reach the source of that infernal drumming that went on and on and on.

'Angus!' A voice from somewhere behind me, snatched away by the wind, but I paid it no notice. I found a tree blown down across my path but vaulted over unthinkingly. The drums were sounding even louder now, thudding above the wind like some lunatic accompaniment. Ahead of me, the path rose and I scrambled up it, my feet sinking into the water-laden sand. I paused at the top and all at once the drums were no longer straight ahead but to my right. I stumbled off the path and almost into the hut I'd known would be there.

I pulled up short. The thing was about the size of a suburban garage, strongly built, with a single window in the side. Directly above where I was standing a loudspeaker poured out God knows how many decibels of drumbeats, like the house music system of a London pub. I put my hand on the wooden planks that made up the wall and felt a steady pulsing. As premises, the building seemed a bit on the small side for the local disco, and besides, no self-respecting disco wastes noise on the night air.

A tearing clap of thunder seemed to split the world in two, blue-white explosions of electricity crackled down towards the horizon, backlighting the trees around me so that the whole world was thrown up in razor-sharp relief. In those instants of flickering light I could see the car coming in from the sea, only this time I could see the shallow raft on which it stood, and the cable that was drawing it steadily in to shore. The cable ended at the hut beside me, and I guessed that if I looked inside I should see a winch with a big twin-cylinder diesel engine alongside the drum that was neatly coiling away the half-mile-long steel cord. I raised my eyes and for just a moment looked beyond the floating car and glimpsed the ship from which it must have been lowered. It was hard to see clearly because of the rain and I didn't have the chance to look for long because at that moment someone hit me very hard on the back of the head and that was that.

Unless one is certifiably dead no one stays unconscious for ever. When I eventually surfaced the storm seemed to have passed but it was even darker than I remembered and I felt like the wrath of God. It's a good dramatic fiction that after a smart bop on the head a character is deemed to be in good working order as soon as he comes round, ready and willing to do what a man's got to do. Not so. I had a headache so monumental that I wouldn't have been surprised if someone had told me my skull was in two halves, and there was a more localized pain somewhere above my right ear that suggested what in court is referred to as 'a contusion' and in novels as 'a lump the size of a pigeon's egg'. Something to explore with tender fingers, had not my hands been tied behind me.

That bastard Gus Aligar. My good golfing companion. My enlightened President. What club had he taken to reach the island? An 8 iron? Presumably that was what he'd clobbered me with. I moved about a bit and beneath me was not sand but boards and uncomfortable strips of metal. Above me the dark was so intense that even my numbed brain could sort out that there was some kind of roof over me that effectively eliminated stars. Also a sweet, tarry familiar scent of oil and petrol. Ergo, I was in the back of some kind of vehicle.

I said aloud, 'That bastard Aligar.' But still my fault
from the beginning. What death wish had prompted me to
go waltzing about in the dark in an area where I'd already
been marked for the chop? What lunatic blank spot had
possessed me to trust His Excellency the President when
all I knew of him was that he liked golf? Well, not all that
much of a blind spot. He'd invited me to visit his bloody
country in the first place, an odd thing to do if he'd been
planning to knock me off. And yet . . .

Outside someone—presumably my guard—was cele-
brating my capture in style with the soft popping of corks.
A brief pause and then someone was pulling aside canvas,
and pitch darkness gave way to a kind of twilight. If I
turned my head I could see out of the truck, at least I
could have done if someone hadn't been standing on the
tailboard, a black shape against the starlit sky.

'God bless all here,' someone said in the tones of County
Meath. 'Are you there now, Mr Straun?'

I said, with difficulty, 'Hello, Birdie.' The great British
understatement, but what else was one to say?

He came over to me, a darker shadow, and got on with
the untrussing. Considering that he was working in near
darkness, he worked with quite remarkable dexterity. Once
my legs were free he pulled me upright. 'Is himself all right,
now?'

Himself? Aligar? Standing up hadn't done my head any
good and it was taking me all my time to keep upright, let
alone think. Then a voice from the far corner said, 'I'm
OK. Get these goddam ropes off me.'

Odd, it had never occurred to me that there might be
anyone in the truck apart from myself, so easy is it to be
self-centred when one's been knocked on the head.

I said, 'Gus—'

'I know. That bastard Aligar. You thought *I* laid you
out?'

I couldn't see him but he sounded as though I'd hurt his feelings. 'Well,' I said, 'yes. There didn't seem to be anyone else about.'

'Some son of a bitch was about all right.'

Birdie said, 'Will ye get outside, now! Quick!' He didn't sound the amiable Irish golf pro we knew and loved. He sounded edgy but he also sounded as though he'd been here before, and we did as we were told. There were two shadows near the rear wheels darker than the rest and Birdie nodded towards them. 'Best get them in the back. We'll not be wanting to leave them lying about.'

One of the shadows was a corporal, the other a private, but both looked equally dead. Well, I'd thought at the time it was an odd place to be hearing corks being drawn and I wondered if Birdie made a habit of going around with a silenced pistol, knocking off such locals as appeared to be getting stroppy. Qualms, possibly, but I did my bit of fetching and carrying and it didn't take long to stow our two guards away in the same place Gus and I had been and the canvas flap tied down.

I looked at Birdie. 'You must have done this before.'

'Sure an' I have, God forgive me. Time an' time again.'

'IRA?'

'Well, it was not the British army, an' we'll be leaving it at that.' Birdie gestured towards the trees. 'Out of sight now, the Captain will be here in a minute.'

Curious the way the basic allegiances of people crop up in unexpected places. *Did you know he was a Mason? A Mormon? An anti-vivisectionist?* Or whatever. With Ireland, it seemed to be the IRA. For terrorists, whatever colour or creed, I held no brief, my Calvinistic forebears darkly at my shoulder. He that liveth by the sword shall die by the sword. And a very good thing too. But one does sad things in one's youth, sometimes, and for all I knew Birdie had been no more than remembering the skills of something

long outgrown. Gus and I owed him, anyway. I said,
'Thanks, Birdie.'

'It's making it quits between us.'

Well, yes. More than quits, actually. I nodded without
speaking.

'How did you find us?' Gus, asking the obvious.

Birdie smiled faintly. 'You'd drink taken, and were
playing a round. It didn't take a wise man to know what
you'd be up to if someone wasn't around to hold your
hand.' He gestured towards the trees. 'Out of sight, now.
It's not here you should be when the Captain comes
back.'

'From where?'

'From finding out from his masters what he's to be doing
with you.'

Only a fool ignores good advice, so we went to ground.
Gus said, 'What masters?'

'God save us, how should I know?' Birdie shrugged his
shoulders. 'It's enough trouble I've been having getting
a golf course ready without botherin' myself with their
troubles.'

I said, 'You bothered enough to kill two men.'

'Sure an' I was owing you a favour.' Birdie O'Shea
turned his head and looked at me. 'Don't be troubling yourself about it. The President here will be telling you it's a
different ball game you're getting yourself into. I've kept
out of it myself, praise be to God, and if you take my advice
you'll do the same. Away back home with you, Mr Straun.'
He turned away from me, listening. 'The Captain's coming
now.'

Gus gave me a push. 'That's it, man. We get the hell out
of here.'

'Stay a bit yet,' Birdie told him. 'Go back of The Ridge
an' he'll be seeing you for sure.'

We stayed. A jeep, running without lights, bumped out

of the trees and pulled up a dozen yards from us and someone in jungle battledress got out. Captain whoever.

Gus said softly, 'If he goes over and apologizes to
those two in there, I for one am going to feel bad about
it.'

The officer took something out of the back of the jeep
and then walked over to the truck. I felt the hair prickle a
little at the back of my neck, a souvenir of my fey grandmother long ago, an uncomfortable gift but sometimes a
useful one. I watched the Captain loosen the canvas cover-
ing the tailboard, toss something inside and walk away
briskly. The grenade blew the back of the truck apart. A
fragment or two must have reached a fuel tank because
fractionally later the front of the vehicle erupted in a great
ball of fire and smoke.

Behind me, Gus said, 'I guess we don't have to ask what
the instructions were.'

I had an uncomfortable memory of myself lying trussed
on the truck's floor. I'd have been a damn sight more
uncomfortable had I still been there when that grenade had
landed. I wondered who it was who had actually said the
words.

Birdie was saying, 'You got a Caddy Car?'

'Yes.'

'You'd better get back in it then, while everyone's
admiring the brew-up.' He was totally unmoved by the
holocaust and I found myself wondering just how many
brew-ups he had seen.

'And you?'

Birdie clearly needed no help from us but one has to ask.
He said, 'I'll be looking after myself.'

I said, 'Before you go—'

Birdie paused. 'You'll be making it brief, Mr
Straun.'

'Yes,' I agreed, 'I'll make it brief. Why?'

'Why am I bothering myself?' He really looked as though he was asking himself the question for the first time, but then who truly understands the Irish?

'Why did you get me out here?'

'Sure and that General Tombi is a terrible man. Hates golf. If he'd had his way here he'd have given it over to tanks, so he would. An' you were the only man I could see the President here asking for help.'

I'd have liked to thank him again but there are some things that if you've said once they're best left alone, and in any case he had already turned aside and was no more than a shadow being swallowed up by the trees. The towering flames from the burning truck were beginning to die down, half a dozen soldiers had appeared from somewhere and were standing with their backs to us, watching the fun. At my side Gus seemed unable to drag himself away, so I dug him in the ribs. 'You coming, or do you want to see the show through again?'

He sighed. Understandably. It can't have been a particularly edifying sight for a head of state. 'Right. Let's get out of here before someone asks us to stay.'

We made our way back to where we'd left the cart. After only a few steps the trees hid the flames so well it was hard to realize there was a fire there at all, let alone that we were supposed to be in it. As we climbed into the runabout I said, 'Well?'

The President shook his head. 'No good looking at me, man. I'm just a part of the crowd.'

'You mean,' I said, 'that you don't know who it was that officer went to for his orders?'

'I do not.'

'And you didn't know about the cars?'

Gus said petulantly, 'I *still* don't know about the goddam cars. I saw one floating on the water just before someone clobbered me. OK, so it's due to end up in Kentola, along with all the other fancy cars. But as to its life story—you tell me.'

I said, 'The car we saw was stolen in Europe, shipped out in a container. Easy enough to ship out that way but a damn sight harder to ship in, because these days *all* containers are being checked.'

Gus looked unconvinced. 'And money doesn't talk any more?'

'Enough money will get anything in,' I admitted, 'but my guess is that enough money is so much it takes the profit out of the deal, so someone thought of bringing cars in where there doesn't happen to be a port. They just unload the car from the ship on to a raft and winch the damn thing in.'

'*Ex Africa semper aliquid novi*,' the President said unexpectedly. 'Always something new out of Africa.'

'Asia, in this case,' I told him. 'It's a trick they were pulling in Sri Lanka back in the 'sixties when they used to float Mercs in there by the dozen.' I hesitated. 'Look, you're absolutely sure you don't know who's behind all this?'

The President fiddled with the steering-wheel. 'Sure I'm sure. But I guess you don't believe that.'

Nobody likes being called a liar, including heads of state. I said cautiously, 'Let's say it seems unlikely.'

'You got to remember I'm a new boy here. This country's just about as strange to me as it is to you. I don't even speak the language, for Chrissake!' Gus looked at me steadily, but then any good con man can look you in the eye.

I said, 'So what have you been doing since you got back?'

'You *know* what I've been doing. Fooling around with my girl and building a golf course.' Then, when I didn't say anything: 'So?'

'So I nearly got shot up there on The Ridge. Brainbridge had already got the report of my death set up, ready to print.'

Gus blinked. 'You mean Brainbridge—'

I shook my head. 'Brainbridge is a newspaper editor,' I said. 'Could be he just prints the news as he gets it.'

'But at least he knows where he got the news *from*.' I waited while Gus sifted through the permutations. He was pretty bright and it didn't take him long to come up with the required answer. 'So by now he should be writing the President's obituary.'

I said, 'Well, he doesn't have to mention your death. Your disappearance maybe.'

The flickering glow in the night sky behind us was growing less, the squall of rain petering out to a few large, warm drops. Gus said, 'We could go and see.'

I was vague about newspaper time-schedules, but it seemed likely that if the news was to get into the morning's edition someone would have to be writing it pretty late. Worth a try, at any rate. 'All right,' I agreed. 'Let's go visiting.'

A Caddy Car is a discreet vehicle, electric motors being both environmentally wholesome and virtually silent. We crossed the golf course and whined out on to the road beyond and into the compound of *The Post*. The building was lit up, presumably signifying that they were in business, so we parked the Caddy Car and went in. At least I didn't have to ask the way to the editor's office, and as the door was open we didn't even have to enter without knocking.

I said, 'Work seems to have called you away from the party.'

As an entrance it would probably have been more effective if we could have managed to disturb an editorial conference, but even so it wasn't too bad. Brainbridge was sitting at his desk admiring a rough copy of what I guessed to be the next day's edition. He looked up when we entered and looked faintly sick. He must have been getting used to

me popping up from the grave but he probably reasoned
that trying the same thing with the local boss man was
likely to be tricky.

He said, 'I thought—'

'We know what you thought,' Gus said. 'Now let's see
what you're planning to tell your readers tomorrow!' He
leaned across the desk and picked up the dummy page.
Brainbridge made no attempt to stop him but by this time
he was looking a good deal worse. When I glanced over
Gus's shoulder I understood why.

PRESIDENT FLEES COUNTRY
WHEREABOUTS UNKNOWN
General Tombi New Head of State

'Bright son of a bitch.' The President managed to infer
a certain appreciation. 'Real bright.' He held the sheet
up so that I could see it better. 'I wonder *why* I ran
for it.'

I said, 'Perhaps Mr Brainbridge could tell us.'

Mr Brainbridge just stood there.

'Please tell us.' The President put the paper down carefully. He didn't sound like the golf club chairman any more.
He sounded as if he could be a real bastard.

Brainbridge kept his mouth shut but he pushed a smaller
sheet across the desk, typewritten this time, but good riveting stuff none the less. It described in brisk terms how
President Augustus Aligar had been unmasked as an
unscrupulous manipulator of public funds who had squan-
dered the nation's wealth in order to maintain a playboy
lifestyle. Unmasked by the incorruptible General Tombi,
he had escaped abroad rather than stand trial.

'So the Army takes over and I'm never heard of again.'
Gus raised his eyes to Brainbridge. 'Who gave you this
crap?'

I had a pretty good idea but rather Brainbridge than me. He hung it out for as long as he could, but he must have been able to tell from Gus's face that delay wasn't a good idea. Finally he said, 'Miss Bouchier.'

The delicious Kiki. The delicious but greedy Kiki. A president would have been good enough for most of her kind, but this one had evidently wanted looks as well.

Gus must have read my thoughts, because he said, 'Good-looking boy, Tombi.'

'As generals go,' I said. I felt bloody sorry for him. The cuckolded lover is the standard object of low farce, but few people who've worn the horns themselves ever get around to laughing.

Gus was prodding the page in front of him. 'When does this edition reach Kentola?'

I suppose it was a relief to get a question that hadn't got a dirty answer. Brainbridge said, 'Tomorrow afternoon.'

'But I imagine General Tombi would like to see a copy before that.' Gus was rubbing his chin again. 'He's in Kentola now. So my guess is you've got a number for him.'

'Yes,' Brainbridge said. He wasn't even trying any more. 'I'm supposed to read the headlines out to him over the phone.'

'Great,' Gus said amicably. 'You do that thing.'

Brainbridge blinked. 'You want me to read them to him *now*?'

The President said reasonably, 'Never mind what I want, Buster. Just do like I tell you.' He really was getting further and further away from the golf club. 'And ask the General when he's coming back.'

The local telephone system seemed to work rather better than the one I'd left behind me because Brainbridge got his number right away.

'General Tombi, please.'

Apparently no General Tombi. Brainbridge switched to

what was presumably Shosi. I was surprised at his fluency, but then he must have been in the country a long time. I wondered if the President was really as ignorant of the language as he pretended to be. Probably not, because human nature prods more people into claiming skills they don't have than the other way around.

Brainbridge put the phone down. 'The General is flying back immediately. He plans to use the beach landing ground as usual.'

I looked at Gus. 'Literally on the beach?' From what I'd seen of it, the beach looked big but not that big.

'It's only a light plane.' The President showed no surprise. 'Tombi fancies himself as a pilot, always flies himself whenever he can. Uses part of the beach as a strip alongside what he calls his Tactical Headquarters.' He looked back at me. 'Maybe we should go meet him.'

'We?' I wasn't sure that I fancied domestic upsets of this nature.

Gus said, 'Sure, all of us. Brainbridge here. You. Kiki. Most definitely Kiki.' He glanced at his watch. 'Flying time for the small plane's about an hour and a half, I believe.'

'Yes, Mr President,' Brainbridge said. 'Just about that.'

'Well, that's nice. Just time to have a few drinks first.' He hesitated. 'Was Colonel Ram still there when you left?'

Brainbridge swallowed. 'Yes, Mr President.'

'Well, that's just great, he can come along, too. You coming, Angus?'

I didn't know what was going to happen in the clubhouse and didn't particularly want to. I said, 'No, I'll just stretch my legs round the corner for a bit. I'll see you at the strip.'

'You know where it is?'

'I'll get Brainbridge here to tell me.'

I walked the course in the dark. How many were in on the car racket? I wondered. Presumably Brainbridge, because he was the local newspaper editor and there would be precious little he didn't know. As for the others, it was hard to say.

In normal circumstances, such as daylight, it's easy enough to fiddle away an hour or so on a golf course whether one is waiting for a partner or the end of an unsuccessful military coup. At night there's not a lot to look at and I was glad when it was time for my return to the fold. I walked up The Ridge to the appointed spot. The committee was hunched together in the shadows of the trees, as if waiting for the show to begin, which I suppose they were.

'Hello, Angus.' The President greeted me much as though he'd come across me in the bar. He nodded towards the dimly visible beach. 'They light it up, same like a proper airfield. Neat.'

'Yes,' I said. I took a glance at Kiki. Her face was expressionless but her eyes were enormous. Come to that, I can't say any of the others looked particularly happy, either.

'Listen,' the President said.

We listened. From somewhere south there was the soft sound of a light aircraft and we all turned towards it. Too dark to make it out but it came on steadily, losing height.

The lights came on.

The lights were portable but they were effective enough. Not enough power to flood the landing area but plenty to outline the boundaries. They didn't make a large rectangle, but then a plane of that size wasn't going to need a lot of space in which to pull up. Perhaps in those moments it seemed to me that the area enclosed by the lights was closer to the land than I'd expected it to be, but of course I hadn't seen the place in daylight so I couldn't be sure. The plane came out of the dark and as it swept past us I saw it was a small Cessna with a tricycle undercarriage. I heard Tombi cut his engine and the little machine dropped neatly down just inside the end of the runway. It bounced once, touched down again, somersaulted once and then exploded into flames.

I said, 'Christ!'

Nobody else said anything at all, they seemed frozen. There didn't seem to be anyone running to the wreck and I suppose there wouldn't have been any point because nothing could have survived. In the light thrown by the blazing petrol one could see quite clearly the six-foot-high sand dune into which the plane had ploughed.

Gus must have been looking, too. 'Someone put the lights in the wrong place,' he said. 'Most unfortunate.'

Colonel Ram, I supposed. It didn't take a lot of guessing that Colonel Ram was likely to be the next Commander-in-Chief, because he was clearly the kind of man who knew which horse to back and when. Good on Colonel Ram. I looked at Kiki. Her face wasn't expressionless now, in fact she looked as though someone had kicked her in the stomach. The others were doing their best to convince themselves that they were somewhere else.

Gus was watching me. I suppose I should have kept my mouth shut but I said, 'You had the lights changed!' Of course he'd ordered the lights changed, it was obvious. But in the circumstances, not much point in going on about it.

The President didn't smile. He said, 'Remember when you told me back at The Rogues about winter rules, Mr Straun?' He didn't wait for me to reply. 'You said they let you do things that would never be allowed in summer, like choosing your own lie. You could get away with murder, you said.'

I didn't say anything.

'Come back in a year and everything will be fine and dandy ' The President wasn't looking at me. He was looking at the pyre that was consuming General Tombi. He nodded, as though remembering something. 'All run according to the book, Mr Straun. But just for now we're on winter rules ourselves. Winter rules, and don't let anyone forget it.'

CHAPTER 15

It was raining when we landed at Heathrow. It was still raining at Tiverton House when I got there and the grey buildings were all in soft focus as I got out of the cab, but in Sergeant Birkin's subterranean retreat it was rather cosy. The place smelled of cars and oil, an odour I found agreeable after the pressurized atmosphere of a big jet, and the coffee Birkin produced from a flask was hot and unexpectedly strong. Ten hours aloft and the sight of an English winter at breakfast-time cracks all but the toughest veneer of civilization and although I neither liked nor disliked Sergeant Birkin he had an ambiance of which I felt in need. I drank his coffee gratefully and tossed him the name of Mike Miller.

'Anything known?'

'No.' Birkin didn't need a computer, he had one in his brain but he couldn't very well produce something that hadn't been programmed. I told him about Gus's Rolls and young Mike's fling with Lady Rosemary. 'Last heard of,' I said, 'he was in the nick at Thornton Basset. I checked on the way here. They let him go.'

Birkin frowned. 'After pinching a Royal Roller.'

I think more to himself than anyone else he added, ''86 Corniche. Hire car. Supplied new by Owen's to Aristo Autorent.'

He wasn't inviting me to be impressed, so I said, 'They let him go because they hadn't much choice. The President wasn't prepared to press charges and Miller hadn't taken anything off the car.'

Birkin sipped coffee. 'So what's the problem?'

'I want to talk to Miller again,' I said. 'He's left his job.

Left home. Apparently nobody knows where he is. I just
thought that if he'd got into any more trouble you'd have
heard about it.'

'Afraid not.' Birkin shook his head and regarded me with
dark, interested eyes. 'What makes this Miller so special?'

I regarded him back. 'I want to know why he's so bad
at his job.'

'I see.' Sergeant Birkin stood a pencil on end with care
and precision. 'Well, keep in touch. I'll put out feelers
among my friends but I'd like to know when I can call them
off.'

'I'll ring you,' I promised. 'I'll be going up to Norfolk in
a couple of days' time to see if I can dredge anything up
from Lady Rosemary. I should be able to let you know one
way or another within a week.'

'*Cherchez la femme*, sir,' Sergeant Endicott said darkly when
I told him. 'You're still officially with the FO. Go and have
a word with that bird of his. Tell her lover-boy's life is in
danger. She'll talk.'

'That horsey lady with a penchant for getting laid by
stable-boys,' Laurie said. 'I bet she knows where Miller is.'

'Endicott had the same idea,' I told her. 'Only he said it
in French.'

'I should jolly well hope so. Sergeant Endicott's the one
person who lends a spot of culture to your sordid crew.'
First evening back, sitting in front of the fire. An electric
fire, but homey for all that. Laurie was on the floor in some
kind of housecoat, fair hair spilling over her shoulders, her
back against my legs. I'd been away less than a week but
it seemed a long time. I shut my eyes for a moment and I
had to open them quickly, but a couple of drams and a
large meal was pretty lethal in my jet-legged state and I
could have slept for a week.

'Are you going to?'

'Am I going to what?'

'See Lady Rosemary Luton.'

'I suppose so.' God, no wonder she admired Joe Endicott, at least he always gave a straight question. 'Yes,' I said, 'I am.'

Laurie twisted her head round and up so that she could look at me. Behind her glasses her eyes were wide with concern. 'Darling, must you? You've done this ridiculous job for the Foreign Office, and it's over. What happens now is none of your concern. And this stolen car business will be sorted out. It's not even your department.'

'That's the point.' If I'd been feeling brighter I'd have thought that much clearer, and logic comes hard when one's only half awake. I said, 'That big ginger bastard who pinched my car. The cocky little sod who took Gus's Rolls. Whoever it was killed Oscar at the garage—they're all linked in some way. Maybe the African end of the car export trade is finished, but I still don't know how it works this end, and I want to find out. Oscar was a good friend of mine. It's personal.'

'You're a policeman, not a private eye. You can't pick and choose your cases.' Laurie was shaking my arm. I found myself thinking that this was a side of her I hadn't seen before.

I said, 'I'm still seconded to Todhunter. If I can stay that way for a few days it'll give me time to dig around on my own.'

'You're out of your mind,' Laurie said despairingly. 'What do you suppose you'll get out of Miller anyway? He's only a kid showing off.'

I said, 'I want to find out who Miller took his orders from. It's as simple as that.'

'He was a joy-rider!' She punched my leg so hard that it hurt. 'He took Gus's Rolls for the hell of it. Why else should he just dump it?'

'Perhaps,' I said, 'because he was told to.' I'd had the
idea kicking around in my mind for some time and it did
me good to say it out loud. 'Birkin insisted there's an
organization that will pinch any car to order. Suppose
Miller worked for it and had been told to pinch a Rolls?
He nicks Gus's and is told that with a diplomat and a
copper riding around in it, that particular one is too hot.
So he drops it like a hot potato.'

Laurie frowned. 'He got tipped off pretty quick.'

'So the car had a phone.'

We sat and looked at the fire. It would have been nice if
it had been a real one with logs falling about, but the fake
flames produced by a little fan somewhere inside the thing
were better than nothing. If you watched carefully you
could catch the same flame coming round.

The Lutons lived in a rather splendid Georgian farmhouse
about ten miles west of The Rogues Club at Thornton Basset. Sir Andrew, according to my informants, had been a
hard-up younger son with an uneconomic liking for horseflesh which had proved something of an embarrassment
for all concerned until he had married Rosemary, elder
daughter of the Earl of Duttington, who had the same tastes
but also the money to enjoy them. Together they had
bought the farm at Ilton St Peter and converted it joyfully
into a home with stables. The farm acres, under professional management, still brought in a healthy return.
The Luton part, all horses and this and that, rather less.
Nevertheless, as a trainer Rosemary Luton's reputation was
by no means bad and I approached her with tact. I could
hardly approach the woman in her own home and question
her about her lover, so in the end I chickened out and
telephoned.

'Lady Rosemary? This is Angus Straun. We met at The
Rogues. Do you think we might have a chat?'

A silence over the phone. Then, 'Of course, darling, I remember you. About what do we chat?'

'One of your staff.'

'Oh.' She sounded disappointed, like a small girl who'd expected a fun present and got something useful instead. Then: 'Do you think it might be better if not here?'

'Much better not,' I said.

'Oh dear.' A hesitation. 'Look, there's a ride through the woods from here that comes out at Plunket's Common. I walk the dogs there sometimes. Would that do?'

'I imagine it would do very well.' We fixed a time and I wondered if she'd be late, which she was not. She was, in fact, five minutes early, looking like a slightly full-blown million dollars in a tweed jacket and cord trousers tucked into wellies. Two shaggy lurchers attended her, padding on tippy-toes.

She didn't greet me, but she smiled with her mouth and eyes, genuine warmth, a rich and likeable slut. 'I suppose it's about Mick Miller.' She was not one to beat about the bush.

'Yes, Lady Rosemary, I'm afraid it is.'

'So?'

'I badly need to speak to him, but he seems to have disappeared. Perhaps you could tell me where I might find him.'

Those wonderful blue eyes surveyed me steadily. 'I don't think so.'

'You don't think you know or you don't think you'll tell me?'

She made a tiny gesture of distress, I suppose at the gaucherie of my asking. She said, 'Whether I know where he is or not is neither here nor there. But if I did I most certainly wouldn't tell you.'

'May one ask why?' I found myself wondering what Sir Andrew might be like. It was inconceivable that he didn't know he was being cuckolded by all and sundry. One could only hope that he had other interests and simply didn't care.

Rosemary Luton answered readily enough. 'The poor boy was being pestered by inquisitive people.'

'So you dismissed him?'

The blue eyes grew frosty. 'Don't be ridiculous! There was no reason for me to dismiss him. I simply sent him somewhere he could get a little peace.'

'Peace from whom, Lady Rosemary?' I asked.

'For the first time she seemed unsure of herself. 'I—I don't know—'

'Newspaper reporters? Policemen?' If I pushed too hard I knew she'd simply tell me to go to hell, but a certain amount of pressure was something I had to risk.

Finally she said, 'Mick was sorry about what happened. He got mixed up with the wrong people. He seemed— apprehensive. I thought it might be a good idea if he had a change of scene.'

'In case he got approached again?'

'Well—yes.' She didn't say, 'Approached by whom?'

I nodded. 'All right. So where is he?'

Rosemary Luton prodded one of the lurchers with her foot. 'I've already said I'm not going to tell you that. And you can't make me.'

I said, 'I expect you've heard the bit about obstructing a police officer in the course of his duty?'

She gave a gurgle of laughter. 'My dear, you can't *prove* I've done anything. And if you try to quote this conversation I'd simply deny it.'

'Oh, that's all right,' I said, 'I expect we can come up with something.'

'Do tell!'

By their confidence shall ye have them. I said, 'He'll still be riding for you in America, I suppose?'

She blinked but didn't say anything, so I went on, 'It's easy enough to find out when. Of course the airport you use for the trip is a routine matter for traffic control. I can have Miller picked up on the way out and arrange to have him questioned for the whole weekend.' I paused and added, 'Shouldn't wonder if we couldn't find some irregularity with your horse boxes, too.'

We looked at each other. Finally she said, 'You really are a bastard.'

'As a matter of fact,' I told her, 'I'm a pretty good-hearted chap, because I can keep Miller out of trouble a good deal better than you can. I give you my word that there'll be no trouble. A few questions and we'll forget the whole thing.'

'You promise?' For a moment she looked extraordinarily vulnerable. Perhaps she really did love the young scamp. In that case she was in for real sorrow, but that was her problem, not mine.

'Yes,' I said, 'I promise.'

'I got Geoff Blunt to find him a job at The Rogues for a few weeks. He cleans tractors for the greenkeepers or something.'

The Rogues! 'God,' I said, 'you didn't send him far.' But then, like the lady said, she wouldn't, would she?

'Far enough,' Rosemary Luton said defensively.

Well, of course, that was a point, too. The woman was so completely overboard about Miller that she'd hardly risk letting him out of her sight. I couldn't imagine that the ground staff at The Rogues would exactly welcome an untrained addition to their number, but on the other hand the lady bountiful had doubtless made it worth somebody's while.

I said, 'He's not living at home. Where does he sleep?' In the circumstances perhaps not quite the happiest way of putting it.

'There's a kind of hayloft to one of the tractor sheds. One
of the greenkeepers used it as an office years ago. He's
camping out there.'

I said, 'Fair enough. How do I get in touch with him?'

Rosemary Luton said without embarrassment, 'I'll be
speaking to him. Where are you staying?'

'The Thornton Arms.'

She nodded. 'I'll see that he rings you there.'

I had doubts, unfounded as it turned out. Miller rang
about six.

'Her Ladyship said you wanted to talk to me, like.'

Did he always call her that? Overtones of Mellors and
Lady C. But then, sex knows no frontiers, the great leveller.
I said, 'Yes.'

'Can you make it after dark?'

Winter in England and it's dark most of the time, but I
told him fine, suit himself.

'She told you where I hang out?'

I remembered seeing the mower sheds during my round
at The Rogues, a series of well-adapted farm buildings
where the course ran parallel with the Thornton road. I
remembered it well because a tractor pulled a scarifier
had passed me as I was making a stroke and the wicked
six-inch-long spikes that aerated the ground had spun
little cylinders of earth all over me. Good greenkeepers
shouldn't do that sort of thing and I'd watched him
balefully as he drove the whole outfit straight into the
confines of the old barn and been swallowed up. There'd
been a dormer window above the ancient entrance. 'Yes,'
I said, 'I know it.'

'Ten o'clock.'

He could have made it earlier and it would still have
been dark but it wasn't a good time to bicker. 'OK,' I said,
'ten.'

*

I'd booked a table at 'Au coin de Thornton Arms' at seven, so I changed it to eight. The traditional old English fare consisted of *quenelles of chicken masked by a discreet rosemary jus,* and proved an experience that needed a couple of over-priced brandies to wash it down, but with the measures having been commensurate with dwarf gnomes, I classed myself as still fit to drive.

It had rained earlier in the day and the East Anglian mists were beginning to fill up the fields. I drove my rented car cautiously towards Thornton Basset but there wasn't a thing on the roads. The lights that illuminated the entrance to The Rogues clubhouse showed up ahead of me and I turned right along the main road. Half a mile further on I could just make out the dark bulk of the mower sheds and at that moment a sliver of moon showed from behind a cloud and I saw that there was a service track leading off the road, rutted with broad tractor wheels. I tucked the Escort behind a hedge where it wasn't likely to be spotted and headed for the sheds on foot.

There's something curiously unsettling about wandering round the countryside in the middle of the night. Wander round the back streets of a city and you get mugged, head off to your neighbourhood beauty spot and you're prey to all the ancient race myths you always said you never believed in. As a small boy I'd seen bogles in the shadow of every tree and I had to tell myself firmly that I'd grown out of them. Laurie, I knew, would have spent the night sitting on the Slaughter Stone at Stonehenge and never given it a thought apart from complaining that it was cold. Angela, that one-time wife of my youth, had once confessed she'd spent a night in a haunted room for some trivial bet, a not over-courageous woman as I remembered, but different.

The huge doors of the mower house were open and there was a light in the dormer window. I glanced at my watch.

Ten o'clock. Was I supposed to wait outside? Presumably
not. There was a rough flight of steps just inside the door,
so I went up. The door at the top was open, light spilling
over my feet.

'Miller?'

Answer came there none. I went inside. There was only
a single room, bare floorboards, old packing cases, a single
bare light-bulb hanging from a rafter and a sleeping-bag
on a camp bed. Nobody there and no place to hide.

'Miller!'

I waited but there was no point in standing there calling
to the dark, so I went back down the stairs and out on to the
edge of the fairway. I tried to remember which one it was.
The sixth? A biting east wind blew a flurry of rain in my face
and I shivered and cursed myself for a fool. What had made
me think Miller would keep his word? There was something
dark out in the middle of the fairway and I walked towards
it, full of an uncomfortable knowledge of what I was going to
find. See one body and you've seen them all. Not true, unfortunately, but true that there's a certain something in
common about the way the dead sprawl, a piece of machinery
caught in motion by the final switch-off.

'Miller—'

I don't know why I spoke out loud because I knew he
wasn't going to answer me. He was on his back, with his
head at an obscene angle, eyes bulging, mouth hanging
open. Poor little sod, no wonder he'd been scared stiff. This
was what he'd been afraid of. I bent down and touched his
face, still warm even in that wind. Someone had broken his
neck simply by gripping the boy's head in his hands, I
could see the livid bruise marks of fingers on the pallid skin.
Someone strong. The hairs at the back of my neck prickled,
and as I stood up a diesel banged into life and from the
black maw of the mower shed a pair of electric eyes flashed
out and began to move towards me.

For a moment I told myself stupidly that it was an odd time to mow the fairway, but then the moon came out again for my benefit and I saw the big tractor sideways as it swung round to miss a tree, saw too that it wasn't pulling a gang mower but the big scarifier. Moonlight glinted on the polished metal spikes as they tore into the ground. The lights centred on me again and the tractor engine bellowed under sudden acceleration. If I'd been Clint Eastwood I'd have shot the driver through the windscreen with a .37 Magnum, but I wasn't Clint Eastwood and I certainly hadn't got a Magnum. Nor anything else for that matter.

I turned and ran.

CHAPTER 16

There is a dreamlike quality about running in the dark. Or near dark, just enough to see where you're going but no more. Run in the light and you run towards something, a finishing line, a tree or whatever. Run in the dark and you run on your own, beyond space and time, heading nowhere. Run in the dark pursued by a tractor towing a few hundred steel spikes and you have the stuff of nightmares. You run for ever and your pounding feet carry you across mown grass that is always the same, while behind a *thing* is breathing down your neck.

At least the tractor's driver had switched his lights off, presumably so that he could amuse himself with me without making a show of it. Probably he could see me well enough, sitting up there—I was wearing a light-coloured jacket that must have shown up like the scut of a speeding rabbit. Meanwhile I was running as fast as I could and knew I couldn't go on much longer. If I slowed, the tractor would be on to me before I had time to catch my breath, but really it made little difference whether I slowed or not because the thing behind me was catching me anyway. I could almost feel it nudging at my shoulder. A pole with a flag marked with a 6 appeared in front of me and I realized I was on the sixth green. I pounded across it and half a dozen strides further on almost fell over the marker for the seventh tee. For some reason I remembered fairly well where I was, but the fact didn't do me much good as I plunged on along the seventh fairway. The thought came to me that the tractor could overtake me any time its driver felt like it, he was just drawing the whole thing out for the fun of it. Run now, die later. Only not very much later.

A man came out of the gloom, waving his arms to attract
my attention, mouth open, yelling something.

'Tricky Dicky! For God's sake, man! *Tricky Dicky!*'

It was Butcher Blunt. I suppose it was a measure of how
far gone I was that I even bothered to recognize him. I
wondered hazily what the Tricky Dicky bit meant. I felt
vaguely that it had meant something a long time ago. It
was what they'd called Nixon. Something else, though.
Christ! *That* Tricky Dicky! The back to front bunker—

If the Butcher hadn't been stabbing an arm towards it
I'd never have found it. Not surprisingly, since the damn
thing was almost invisible from this direction in daylight,
let alone the dark. But suddenly, there it was, at my feet.
The Butcher vanished somewhere away to my left, reasonably enough, because there was no tractor actively chasing
him. Me, I went over the edge and dropped the full six feet.
The tractor must have been really incredibly close at the
time because it made no attempt to stop and just carried
straight on. It was like watching one of those war films,
where the hero huddles in a ditch while panzers roll over
the top of him, because there I was at the bottom of that
bunker looking up. The tractor took it like a steeplechaser,
landing on the far side with the most godawful crash that
rocked the world. The moon chose that moment to come
out again and in its light I saw the whole thing. If the
tractor had been fitted with a cab things might have been
different, but it wasn't and the shock of landing threw the
driver overboard like a sack. It was Ginger. I could even
see the look of horror on his face, but not for long. The
tractor plunged on and the scarifiers followed. Ginger vanished beneath them.

I said, 'Jesus!'

I don't know whether he screamed or not because at that
moment there was a lot of metal making a lot of noise,
but he certainly wasn't saying anything by the time the

greenkeeper's toy had passed on. Without a driver the tractor slowed to a chugging crawl and I saw Butcher Blunt
jump up and switch the engine off. Then I straightened up
and he came back and we both had a look at what was
left.

'Haven't seen anything like that since—quite a long
time.' I suppose Blunt wasn't called Butcher for nothing.
After one quick glance I took slow deep breaths and made
haste to think of something else, but my companion pon-
dered the scene with professional interest. 'Twenty-seven,'
he was counting to himself. 'Twenty-eight. That one smack
through the eye—'

I said, 'Shut up, for Christ's sake!'

He smiled grimly. 'Sorry. Takes one back, though.'

I said, 'Thanks anyway.' I nodded to the thing on the
grass. 'About him. I thought—' I stopped. In the circumstances it wasn't going to be tactful, what I thought.

'You thought Bothma was still working for me?' Blunt
looked genuinely surprised.

'Bothma?'

'Piet Bothma. I believe he called himself Boothman latterly but he started out Cape Dutch.'

'When he was a mercenary with you,' I said.

Blunt nodded. 'You noticed him in the picture in my
office, I suppose.' He shrugged. 'It took all sorts in those
days. All sorts. A lot of them weren't half bad, but not the
way they were painted. Must admit Bothma was one of the
bad ones. Strong. Christ, he was strong! I've seen him do
things you wouldn't believe. Some things you wouldn't *want*
to believe. But psychotic. Violent. Mad.'

'You kept in touch?'

'After the mercenary business was played out?' Blunt
shook his head. 'Bothma looked me up a couple of times.
Wanted to know if I knew of anything going in his line.
Had to say no. True, too. Volunteer armies had too much

bad press for my liking. Good fun while it lasted but enough is enough.'

I found myself believing him. There must be plenty of survivors around who've known rough, tough days but have no particular desire to go back. I asked him how he'd known I'd been up for the chop that night.

He said promptly, 'Rosemary Luton told me. Apparently Bothma called at her place looking for Miller. Of course the silly bitch is convinced nobody knows about what's going on, whereas everyone on her payroll knows the score. Bothma shook Miller's address out of some stable-boy, who subsequently told Rosemary, who got in a right old panic and phoned me. Don't suppose she was over-worried about you but she was out of her mind about Miller.' He paused. 'Have you seen him, by the way?'

'Yes,' I said, 'I've seen him. Ginger—Bothma—got to him first.'

'God! Poor old Roz.'

'Yes,' I said, 'poor old Roz.'

I drove back to London next morning. To London, to London to buy a fine pig. Nobody should drive to London with a light heart leaving two corpses behind him, but I was relieved that Ginger Bothma was out of the way. Criminal investigation should by rights be an objective business and the pursuit of truth isn't helped when the investigator feels that at any moment he himself may become another statistic. But I recognized the euphoria that divides the living from the dead and drove circumspectly to Tiverton Street, twenty-four hours left in hand.

Sergeant Endicott was waiting for me, looking expectant.

'All right, Sergeant, let's have it.' One could always tell when Endicott thought he was on to something, his dark face fairly glowed with anticipation. What was it this time?

'Sergeant Birkin's file is on your desk, sir. You asked for it.'

Yes, so I had, but it wasn't going to do Joe much good. I was within my rights to call for a personal file if I felt like it, but I had no intention of divulging its contents to even the most faithful of henchmen. Endicott might have the darkest of suspicions regarding David Birkin but I certainly wasn't going to confirm them for him. And anyway, there could hardly be anything very hair-raising in the file or Birkin wouldn't be holding his present job.

I opened the sealed envelope and took out the file and leafed through it. Birth, education, record of service. The comments of suitable authorities, duly initialled from time to time.

Birkin, David Leigh. b. Leeds. 1.6.61. British
Father: James Leigh Birkin. b. Marlow, Bucks. 1.7.30. British. Draughtsman. Served R.A. (Sergt) Korean War. Died: Dorchester. 7.2.84 (traffic accident.)
Mother: Patricia Jane Birkin, nee Burchall. Born, High Wycombe, Bucks, 17.8.31. British. Secretary, Halifax Building Society.

I read on, but it was all much as one might have expected, a background so unremarkable that it was probably interchangeable with the records of scores of other police officers throughout the country. Maybe David Birkin's school record was rather better than most. As a youngster he'd collected a lot of O levels and ended up at the local Grammar School where he'd played most sports and captained the First Fifteen. Academically bright, he should have gone on to University but instead spent a year travelling. At the age of nineteen he was back in England working in a small engineering firm. By the time he was twenty-one he'd joined the Police.

A quite exceptional recruit. Keen, hard-working and with a quick grasp of detail.

An officer who is not afraid to use his own initiative but never goes beyond reasonable grounds.

Birkin's memory is phenomenal and he puts it to good use. A promising officer who should go far.

The comments of his superiors were as one. Thumbs up for Birkin, a coming man. Not even the old snide remark which might have suggested that someone thought he was a bit whiter than white.

I felt Endicott's eyes on me.

'He's clean,' I said without looking up. 'No problems.'

I went on reading, as much to avoid meeting those reproachful brown eyes as anything else. Personal files can produce odd bits of information quite apart from a subject's religious observances. David Birkin owned a cottage near Dorking, at least it was called a cottage. Apparently cars were his main interest off duty as well as on, because he was a full member of the RAC, similarly the Railton Owners Club. Railtons were rare beasts dating from the middle 'thirties. I vaguely recollected that they'd been cooked up by an English firm using a straight eight American Hudson engine and, like most anything else from that era, changed hands today at some ludicrous price.

For a time I kicked around the fact of a police sergeant owning that kind of car. Presumably there was a similar note about Inspector Angus Straun running around in a Maserati, but then I'd a few reasonably well-known books to show where the money came from. On the other hand, a single sergeant wasn't exactly on the breadline these days and in any case Birkin could well have bought his toy a few years back when the market was rock bottom. Only canny

Scottish Inspectors frittered their money away when it was at an all-time high.

I pushed Birkin's file back in its envelope and re-sealed it. Something was knocking at the back of my memory but for the life of me I couldn't think what.

It was my last day with the Foreign Office as my master and I couldn't wait to be off. Adrian Todhunter had invited me to lunch but I couldn't face a club again so I told him I'd see him in his office, and ate steak and kidney in a pub with Laurie instead. Like so many ideas that seem good at the time, this was reasonably disastrous, the once rather pleasant dining-room rocking to the sound of canned music and London's commercial artisans getting stoned out of their minds in the bar below.

'For God's sake,' I said, 'how do they work in the afternoon with gin running out of their ears?'

Laurie said practically, 'Some of the world's greatest literature was written by chaps with gin running out of their ears. Or laudanum, or whatever. Don't be so touchy.'

'It's my age.'

'I thought maybe it was, too, but I didn't like to mention it.' She gathered her things together. 'What time are you saying goodbye to your friend Todhunter?'

'Half past two.'

'I'll walk with you across the park.'

We walked across St James's Park, beneath the bare trees. In summer the benches would have been full of lovers and office workers eating sandwiches and dropping crumbs for the pigeons, but the fine drifting mist kept them empty now.

Laurie said, 'What's the matter?'

'Frankly,' I said, 'I don't know.' Though frankly I did. The criminal returning to the scene of the crime syndrome. I'd felt guilty about snooping on Birkin and I'd gone down to be matey to him. As it happened, he wasn't there. I'd stood around for a couple of minutes and was just about to go when I'd seen this vintage car magazine on his desk.

'You pinched it?'

'No,' I said, 'I just picked it up and looked at it. There was a section for one-make car clubs, reporting events— that sort of thing. There was a picture of a get-together of the Railton Owners' Club. It said twelve Railtons had turned up, a Terraplane and a Brough Superior.'

Laurie looked up sharply. 'Charlie Brown's got a Brough Superior. But you always said it was a motorcycle.'

I said, 'I always *thought* it was a motorcycle. The Brough Superior was supposed to have been the finest bike ever made. Lawrence of Arabia was killed riding one. But I couldn't see the magazine making a mistake over a thing like that, so I rang up the club secretary. Apparently after he'd given up making bikes Brough produced a few cars with the same name.'

Laurie shrugged. 'So Charlie Brown's got a car called a Brough Superior instead of a motorcycle. Big deal. Though I still don't see why a thing called a Brough belongs to some other make's club.'

I said, 'It's because Railtons and Broughs and Terraplanes all used American Hudson engines.'

'So?'

'So Charlie Brown and David Birkin both belonged to the same club. I checked. The club's a very small one, so they must have known each other?'

'Darling,' Laurie said, 'I'm being very thick. But why does it matter?'

'I don't know yet.'

'Well, you won't be able to ask Charlie about it. He and Alice left this morning for their place in the Bahamas.'

I stopped dead. 'Are you sure?'

Laurie said, 'Of course I'm sure. Alice gave me a handful

of her Cilla Black CDs. You know, the ones she was always playing? I thought that was sweet of her.'

Alice Brown, with her passion for the 'sixties. Cilla Black and the Beatles and the whole Merseyside scene. I said, 'I don't suppose she'll want them back.'

Laurie shook my arm none too gently. 'Would you mind telling me what's going on?'

A couple of the park's mallards flew low level past us with a clatter of wings, and I watched them until they were out of sight. Most things drop into place if you push them around enough, but it's still a surprise when they do.

'Tonight,' I promised her, 'I'll tell you tonight. I don't want to keep Todhunter waiting.'

He'd moved his office since my last visit and his new one was larger, with a better carpet and a view of the park. I didn't want coffee but it came just the same. He must have gone up in the world because it was in a pot this time, with a little jug for the cream.

Todhunter wasn't exactly smiling but was by no means far off it. He said, 'You know, I really think the Chakra business went off quite well. Everyone's very pleased.'

I sipped the coffee cautiously but I need not have worried because it wasn't very hot. I said, 'I'm glad about that.'

Todhunter leaned forward. 'Has Aligar really got a golf course out there?'

I said a bit blankly, 'Yes. It'll be a very good one. What made you think he hadn't?'

'I got the impression President Gus was more interested in getting someone to give him a helping hand with his internal affairs than advice on golf. We couldn't send any of our chaps, of course, would have been most improper. But you seem to have coped with that fellow Tombi quite splendidly. I liked the business of moving his plane's landing lights.' Todhunter really did smile this time. 'Was that your idea?'

'No,' I said, 'I haven't graduated to assassination yet.'

I don't think Todhunter heard me because he was saying, 'It's a pity he couldn't have got rid of that dreadful girl-friend of his at the same time. Still, there's always tomorrow. What did you think of her?'

I said, 'I think she was on to me. At least, she tried to put a bullet through me when we were playing at The Rogues.'

'Did she now!' Todhunter looked interested. 'Are you sure?'

'Pretty sure. She carried a remarkably large golf bag. I suspect she had a rifle in it.' I remembered that at the time of the shot Kiki had been by herself among those trees, ideal cover for someone with a silenced rifle. I'd been lucky to get away with it.

Todhunter said curiously, 'Why you, when she could have shot the President instead?'

'Because,' I told her, 'Kiki had got her horse backed both ways. She'd already got one president and had an option on the next. I don't imagine for a moment that she believed I was just a simple minder and I was too interested in stolen cars for her liking.'

'Ah, the stolen car racket out there.' Todhunter nodded. 'Of course that'll fizzle out now that Tombi's gone. One thing I don't understand, though.'

'Tell me,' I said. 'I'll try to help.'

'Well, when Tombi had got a car ashore, exactly how did he get it out of Chakra and into Kentola?'

I said, 'He used a troop transporter. Personnel carriers went across the border regularly because the two armies did combined training exercises. They're big vehicles. Quite big enough to take a car.'

Todhunter looked pleased. 'Very neat and tidy.'

I said, 'There's still this end to clear up.'

'Well, ye-es.' Todhunter stroked his tie to see that it was properly tucked into his mustard-coloured waistcoat. It was. 'You've been doing a little clearing up on your own account, I hear.'

I didn't bother to ask how he knew, because he wasn't going to tell me and it would be naïve not to suppose that my masters and his didn't work hand in glove. I said, 'A thug called Piet Bothma got himself killed, yes. But he wasn't the man behind the stolen cars for Africa racket.'

Todhunter raised his eyebrows. 'Indeed? And I suppose you know who was?'

I said, 'I think it will turn out to be Sir Charles Brown.'

The Foreign Office stopped fiddling. 'What makes you think that?'

What indeed? I poured myself some more coffee and wondered how much was going to be provable in court. With enough effort, I guessed, a good deal. I said, 'The trade in stolen cars is enormous, and so is the market. Brown knew Africa, he knew there was a ready market in Kentola, so he arranged for high value stolen cars to be shipped to the coast of Chakra, hauled ashore on rafts, and then transported in to the customers.'

I saw that Todhunter was about to break in but I stopped him. 'Brown knew that some kind of investigation was being carried out, so he *asked* me to check on the obvious channel—the arrivals, which he knew were in the clear.'

'Proof?'

'Bothma stole my car but crashed it, so he had to find a replacement. He found one at the garage I use, although he had to kill the chap there to get it. It all seemed pretty horrific because the body was stuffed into one of those big stoves garages use, but to someone of Bothma's mentality it was simply somewhere to get the body out of the way.'

Todhunter nodded. 'Go on.'

I said, 'Another of Brown's employees, Miller, stole Gus
Aligar's Rolls because it happened to fit an order, but when
he rang Brown on the car phone to say that he'd got it, he
was told to drop it because it was too hot. That's why Gus
got his car back still as good as new.'

'And that mayhem at the Rogues the other night?'

I said, 'I knew Miller could tell me who was running the
business, so I went to see him. Brown knew I was planning
to drive to Norfolk and guessed why, so he sent Bothma to
keep him quiet. I imagine you know the rest.'

Todhunter wasn't fiddling with his tie any more. He said,
'You keep saying Brown knew this and knew that. *How* did
he know you were going to Norfolk? How did *you* know that
Miller spoke to him on Gus's car phone?'

'Our own Stolen Vehicles expert, Sergeant Birkin, told
him,' I said.

Todhunter blinked. 'You mean he accidentally let the cat
out of the bag?'

'He let quite a few cats out of bags in his time,' I told
him. 'But not accidentally.' I thought of the couple of hours
I'd just spent with Birkin. I went on, 'He's a brilliant police
officer, probably irreplaceable, but unfortunately — '

'Bent?' Todhunter prided himself on picking up the
jargon.

'Flawed, yes. Bent — ' I shrugged. 'Depends on how you
look at it. The way I see it, Birkin started off with two
things against him. One, he was gay; two, he likes nice
things he couldn't really afford. He had a thing about vintage cars, which was how he met Charlie Brown. They both
belong to the Railton Owners' Club. Charlie was rather
like my Sergeant Endicott—he could spot someone who
was gay in five minutes. Eventually he blackmailed Birkin
into giving him the odd titbit of information about the
whereabouts of certain cars. Probably not much but enough
to be useful to someone in Brown's line of business. Birkin

claims that he thought it was no more than a social inquiry when he was asked about my whereabouts the last few days.'

Todhunter said, 'But my dear chap, you can't blackmail people for being gay these days. I understand that for some jobs it's almost a qualification.'

Well, yes. 'Brown wasn't going to report Birkin to the police,' I told him. 'He was going to tip off Birkin's intended bride, who happens to be very wealthy indeed. He rather needs her to maintain his lifestyle. I gather he's already heavily in debt.'

'Poor devil.' Todhunter could be unexpected at times. 'What'll happen to him?'

I said, 'I think he'll be allowed to resign quietly, no questions asked.'

'And he'll marry the girl?'

'Well—yes.' I hadn't thought about that. 'Could be the making of him.'

'I wouldn't count on it,' Todhunter said. 'Now tell me about the phone.'

'Nobody can leave car phones alone,' I told him. 'Kids steal cars and ring up their Mums. I just punched the re-dial button to see whose number Miller had called. It was Brown's.' Strictly not true. In fact, all I'd heard was a woman's voice with a Liverpool accent. All I *thought* I'd heard. In fact I now realized it had been Alice Brown with a background of her eternal Cilla Black I'd been listening to. All very circumstantial, nothing to do with Todhunter.

We looked at each other. What I'd said had made sense to me and I didn't particularly care whether Todhunter agreed or not, because nothing was going to alter the fact that he was Foreign Office and I was Police.

Finally he said, 'You've not explained why a distinguished man such as Sir Charles Brown should risk his reputation for the sake of a few stolen cars. The man's already a millionaire several times over.'

I remembered Charlie Brown's wild economies and his inability not to make a profit, however small. 'Frankly,' I said, 'I don't think the man could help himself. If there's money going, he's just got to have it.'

Todhunter nodded. 'I agree. The man's a kleptomaniac.'

I blinked. 'Truly?'

'Oh yes. Has been for years. His wife spends half her life going round shops and paying up after him. All the stores know him, of course. They're very understanding.'

Everyone had known, except the people most concerned. Oh well. I said, 'He's in the Bahamas at the moment, but we'll get a case out against him by the time he comes back.'

'He may not come back,' Todhunter said. 'And if he does, I think you'll be advised, nay instructed, not to bring charges against him.'

I put down my coffee cup. 'For God's sake,' I said, 'the man's committed murder!'

Todhunter looked pained. 'Of course he hasn't. Bothma committed murder, and Bothma's dead. Fortunately. Really, my dear Straun, Brown's a national benefactor—charities worldwide. Half the Third World considers him the representative of British compassion. You can't seriously think we'd jeopardize all that just because he let himself get involved in a sordid car racket?'

I stood up and walked over to the window, because suddenly there didn't seem to be much air. I said pointlessly, 'The man's a crook and the law's the law.'

I heard Todhunter sigh. If you prick us do we not bleed? Perhaps even Foreign Office officials bled at times. Behind me he said, 'You're a golfer, Straun. Aren't there things called Winter Rules?'

Gus had said much the same thing, I remembered. 'Yes,' I said, 'you can get away with murder under Winter Rules.'

I stared down at the park below Todhunter's window. The lights were coming on and a cold grey mist was settling beneath the skeleton of the trees.

There was a girl standing under one of the lamps, stamping her feet with the cold, one hand clutching that inevitable bag of books. God knows how long she'd been there.

'Spring,' Todhunter was saying sympathetically, looks like being a little late this year.'

Laurie was looking up. She must have seen me because she raised a hand. 'Oh, I don't know,' I said.